T0199111

Brian Miller: Joan of Arc and the Dragon-Stars

Brian Miller:
Joan of Arc and the Dragon-Stars

Book Six

J. Michael Brower

BRIAN MILLER: JOAN OF ARC AND THE DRAGON-STARS BOOK SIX

With illustrations or photos by:
Rachel Brower, Leah Brower and Symantha Smith

Acknowledgement:
For Rosemarie Skaine

The image of Joan of Arc gratefully adopted from the Ann Arbor Paperback by the same name, written by Jules Michelet, 1967.

iUniverse books may be ordered through booksellers or by contacting:

iUniverse
1663 Liberty Drive
Bloomington, IN 47403
www.iuniverse.com
1-800-Authors (1-800-288-4677)

Because of the dynamic nature of the Internet, any web addresses or links contained in this book may have changed since publication and may no longer be valid. The views expressed in this work are solely those of the author and do not necessarily reflect the views of the publisher, and the publisher hereby disclaims any responsibility for them.

The stories, and goings-on herein are entirely fictional in this publication (for now) and all the related elements are trademarked by the author, so couldn't be colluded to include unsolicited submissions of ideas, stories, artwork, or, indeed, other-such goings-on.

Any people depicted in stock imagery provided by Getty Images are models, and such images are being used for illustrative purposes only. Certain stock imagery © Getty Images.

ISBN: 978-1-5320-6111-0 (sc)
ISBN: 978-1-5320-6112-7 (e)

Print information available on the last page.

iUniverse rev. date: 10/31/2018

Contents

Chapter Sub-Zero

Jeanne la Pucelle Must Not Die!

—**D**on't you see, my strapping and illustrious Dragon-Stars? Agreed, we should leave Earth. I admit Katrina and I lost that fight to get saurians to stay on this planet. It's best that all of us, companions and dragons, just go. That's keeping with anarchy, and I'm not trying to get full-Thoreau or Guy Fawkes on you noble saurians, no. Now, this is something Googleable, too, so fact-check-the-shit-out-of-me! Dracula and Joan of Arc are <u>both</u> together in the year 1431! One was born, one died! The Devil and a Saint in the same year, so, before we leave the Earth, we've got to go back in time to save Jehanette! That's the answer to the saurian question *why* aren't we leaving Earth now? Vlad the Impaler, born under a dragon, was Dracula. My lords and ladies, I don't think the planet needs to know my opinion for world improvement, but it desperately desires Joan of Arc! Here, a young Alligatorian, Anakimian, at this Not-table, he's rightly her companion, he <u>should</u> be rescuing her, saving her. She is a teenager, 19, and should lead the new 30 companions! Leadership has fallen from me, I'm a little controversial. Like Littorian, I never wanted it *anycare*! I implore you, my saurians, to save this

Herold of God!¹ Softly screaming and gently yelling, this is how

---

¹ The noble reptilians sitting round were painstakingly gathered by me. They were 'right in the middle' of leaving the Earth when I interrupted them! I was frankly overjoyed to be in such company, although, I'm afraid, some saurians really disliked me—Danillia for one. The 'alien camp or club' was like a little reptilian city, everything made of wood, intricately designed. The Black World weapons made this place paradise, and 'wood' (even ironwood!) was at their every command. It was a lot nicer than Larascena's Arc, but I'm hiding that from Lara, leaving it in a footnote, hoping that gets overlooked. Every structure, so pristine, so formulated in a saurian way, well, it was just CGI-gone-Manson! The easy-going-nature of the reptilians just sitting around like the Egyptian sphinxes just overwhelmed the entire event. The Table-Not-There, had everyone sitting as a sphinx (Jing was a contortionist and could sit in a saurian-way), all of them at sixes-and-sevens given my sudden announcement. And, regarding the 'summoning' of everyone, I don't mean 'ordered' or even really 'suggested' it was just this: Larascena, the Warlord of Alligatoria, and Clareina, the youthful Lizardanian, helped me get everyone there. Both of these saurians were my wives, not that this means anything outside of (just) us. My saurian wives were free to do whatever they wished, they had absolute freedom, there were no marriage vows—I accepted saurian anarchy, even wrote a book on it. (Incidentally, at this meeting, a pile of my books covered an insignificant part of the Not-table. Everyone alien was imitating some sort of a Velociraptor-on-steroids, but I've described them over-much. They were so noble looking, physically quite unbelievable. Now some saurians thumbed through my books and did their traditional head-wobbling-thing. "Geezum crow, did he just say "cucumber"? Is that some sort of symbolism, what's that supposed to represent? Oh, I get it now, this is--Wow, I've never seen the like, is this art or just-extreme-yuck?" I noticed that on the 'sexually explicit' chapters, though, despite the little, light criticisms I got, some reptilians had their

I communicate with saurians about something so important!

I said it all rapidly, knowing the attention span of both dragons and teenagers was about the same. This took me 37 seconds to say, but my pounding on the Not-table (the floor, installed by the Black World weapons was ironwood, from Australia, the hardest

---

mouths appreciably watering. I'd be the first to say that 'mistakes are made' in my books, but really, I don't care much at all.) I took that 'watering bodacious behavior' as a complement and winked at my wives. Also, around the Not-table, in addition to my betrothed, were Teresian and her brother Kukulkan (both Wysterians—it was really fun to hear their enthusiastic, and bold, conversations ((said and telepathically)) about their other-worldly adventures—and quite obviously they wanted to get Ivan, Kukulkan's companion, and Katrina off Earth just so instantly! With their Wysterian-powers-super-unimaginable they'd doubtless succeed). Too, Kerok, the wisest Alligatorian, was also there (and I'd rather give all my thought and life away to Death Incarnate in exchange for one hour of Kerok's kindly, and understanding, counsel). Also, we had Littorian, Lord of the Lizardanians, Soreidian, Littorian's second (Mr. Joe Triassic in my first book) Danillia (as a shape-shifter she was Leah Starblue, and maintained her role as Soreidian's real assistant), Turinian, Lord of the Crocodilians, and Terminus, Turinian's second. Danillia I really had a fear for, and she cracked her enormous sinewed knuckles knowingly at me, flashing her razor-myriad teeth). I'd always have something to fear from that Lizardanian! Danillia did look respectfully (but grudgingly) at my wives, though. The teenage humans at hand were Katrina Chakiaya, Sheeta Miyazaki, Jing Chang, Rachel Dreadnought, Jason Shireman and Ivan Chakiaya. I heard some comments about me, kinda shitty complaints. I don't know who dissed me, but I can guess, the voice was male. And since there is no 'authority' in anarchy, no one remembers one dying king (that'd be me), and with Joan of Arc coming, dispatching my 'honorary' role, I guess I was my <u>own</u> fading and lingering, *Lion in Winter*.

wood known) caused some consternation. I just blasted my words out. The reason is that Joan of Arc is the most notable human being ever (in my opinion, of course).

You see, the "new" 30 companions needed a leader and I had kind of a bad reputation. Being the companion to the "head dragon" didn't do any good in the world of anarchy. The new 30 were acquired after the dreadful events caused by Genotdelian, the previous Lord of the Crocodilians. I did have some 'interaction' with Genotdelian and tried to appease him. My draconic-diplomacy draconianly failed, and it ended, well, a little badly (for me). Leadership had fallen, but Jeannette could do what failed me.

Anarchy was the political attitude of the dragons (that is, they held <u>no</u> political attitude). The saurians couldn't stay here, that was plain. Joan of Arc (as the English called her) <u>could lead</u> all of us to a 'higher' place (again, setting anarchism aside). Tiperia was standing all alone at the far end of the Table-Not-There, all-my-saurian-sphinxes in utter shock (and awe!). No one said word-one. I was kinda used to this deafening response.

The Crocodilians were my ace—and the Asians could handle that, I had confidence in them. And calling those two 'Asians' isn't a racist term, it was a blanket term. In that 'blanket' I'd be safe. It's a gift, I know I know, stop your clapping, I don't need a round-of-a-hand.

Alternatively, I recognized I'm no saint or anything near it. Leadership was not for me. Littorian had a problem with 'overall direction' anyway, that cried against anarchism. I grew up in the city and have some 'unique' ways, so saurians say I'm into offending people. I think folks should be more tolerant otherwise I'll leave, and that toot-sweet!

Of-a-sudden, Soreidian spoke, interrupting my broken-down train of near-thought.

—Wow, putting a spark to a bridge, right, Brian? That's just like you. I do think this human is just insanely-ass-talking. However, I <u>do</u> agree with him, I think I will attend and support a rescuing of Joan of Arc. Just shut your cake hole, Brian, this isn't the narcissism of 'minor difference,' I'll just explain, damn your so Hollywood all the time, and I'm not going to do the word-parsing and language-policing that you do when speaking to us! One thing, instantly talking isn't really communicating, my troublesome human, and desperately talking is dangerous. Consider the company you're in. I'm also disturbed about this phantasm-of-companionship between Littorian and Brian but set that aside. This rescuing of Jeannette is the last act, before the saurians can really go. This country, America, is all for war, that's why you can't have nice things. The Lord of the Lizardanians can support this final deed, right Littorian? As peace arrives, your moniker of Lord of the Lizardanians comes into question. I'm sure you realize the same. Maybe, then, the friendship between Littorian and Brian can go quietly into the night or just be strangled in my willing claws?[2] We'll see.

---

[2]   Soreidian and I went back a long (or short) way and it was a very rocky relationship. He was a bit 'hunger,' 'more-gargantuan,' just another over-ripped Velociraptor, a little more cleverly 'toned' than Littorian. At one point in our meeting, and this is something I'll expose just this one time, Soreidian said he did see Jamie Johnson's _The One Percent_. Capitalism rules all the Josey Wales' that you have out there—that is to say, in his opinion, all humans were bad (with certain companions and some Russians separated out). Then he said all saurians rest their case with _The One Percent_. I did try to 'get along' with Soreidian but I think Rachel and Jason didn't want me in their kinda-class. Soreidian said we don't even have 'democracy' in America, just a military-industrial complex, secret societies, all of that runs America and he was uncomfortable

I looked over at Rachel and Jason, with my bagel mouth.

---

living in the United States. If an individual 'gets too big' they just assassinate him/her/them. "These humans are such a wacky bunch!" All the saurians agreed with this assessment. The ends don't justify the means, no bloodletting can ever emerge humanity as something angelic. At one point, Soreidian, in marked cruelty (even for him) said this. He was harking back to <u>The Theory of Saurian Anarchy</u>. What was Marx <u>wearing</u>? What was Engels <u>wearing</u>? When I just responded with a dumb look, he said they were 'behaving' as bourgeois, sporting their style of clothes, because the bourgeois had won everything, and maybe for all time. Lenin was the same, very stylish as a bourgeois-in-dress. Only Mao and Stalin dressed as what they'd become, a plain uniform and dictatorship was the result of their 'plainness.' Soreidian was keying on Marx, but he didn't mention him before, at least, not that I know of right-then, but he probably referenced his work (or Hegel's work), which I had on a conference Not-table during our meeting on rescuing Joan of Arc. Soreidian essentially agreed with the saurian-line on Marx and socialism. For me, I have been diffident, and irresolute over my Champaign communism. Soreidian, then, saw humanity as weak. All the premises of Marxism are so wrong, he said, its internally inconsistent, based on those wrong-headed notions—look at *real life* and frail-humanity's-so-brief-reign! The enemies have to be preserved and persuaded, but not arrested, not Guillotined. In my opinion, we can have 'humanitarian-Lizardanian-ness' after final victory. As Edward Bernstein said, the process is everything, the final end, nothing at all. You can't 'force' people (or saurians) into anything. To Soreidian, human terror is 'just justice.' I think that's an insane way to go. My companion's way is much better. (Oh, and if my companion wasn't there ((and my wives, too)), I would have been tossed into the Seine by Soreidian (((with limbs dutifully cleaved off by Soreidian's handsome claws, I'm sure)))). Holy hell, that's not the introduction to France that I'd be wanting to make, like, no way!

They looked calculating, a tad sinister, both wryly smiling. Seeing this coming, I was Mac-trucked-splatted. I recovered and looked around the circular Not-table with a slight smile.

–I do enjoy my talks with Soreidian, he's the definition of an enstrengthened, ultra-post-muscled god. He has a 'functional meanness' rare among dragons-of-anywhere. I know I can ride him anytime I feel like visiting any fast-food place like McAssholes. Whatever's next!

Soreidian was most equal to my (now seized back and dragonized) moment.

–I tolerated you on your last book, about anarchy. I understand a companion did your original cover design? Uh-huh. I guess no one can really do a saurian-right (artistically). Well, unless you get someone really professional, like a Japanese anime guy or gal, maybe then. I did share your mind, during our fight with those stupid mechanical dragons on Carcosa. I see why Littorian likes you. Maybe we'll have our ultimate confrontation on this rescuing of Joan of Arc, okay, Brian? I'd squash 'n' jellyize you, but good. And like Littorian says, you can't impugn intent, and that means condemning human ignorance. Yes, <u>you</u> can't. <u>But I can!</u>

At that, Jason and Rachel giggled. Jason fired at me, both 10-gauge-barrels. Talk about piling-on, shit, brother.

–What's got you looking toe-down, Brian? You're guilty without saying anything, just like any famous American. I'm a companion, and I know this to be true: If you get famous, there is a throw-down eventually, you should know that by now. The media, the social press, they'll find some scandal. Leadership must have a fall. And you also know what they say, 'It is easier for a poo-bird to go threw the eye of a needle than a rich human to give a shit.' The fact that God is dead is so yesterday. And the sooner we're out of here, the far-better. I'm tired of humans, and I know my eventual fate, and I'm looking forward to being a dragon! Can you stand that fate? I can. As you know, the 'reasons' for our rich 1% to 'justify' their wealth are hopelessly lost on by the other 99% because the poor just don't understand that rational minds have to rule over their irrational impulses. The 99% doesn't even give a shit anyway, and if they want to make 'something better' they end up with dictatorial-style communism or hopeless socialism! Companions like you are hoping to impress the saurians, but you're over-matched. The Earth is a lost-cause, and that at close-out prices. I hope Joan of Arc will see the reality of what I say, even if you don't. And you don't.

Jason had his hand on my shoulder, then.

−Get off me scumbag. Your comments are ignorant of the Nordic countries, just by the way, you'd better do some more research. Your 'ignorance' justified. You can't even conceive what they have accomplished under democratic socialism because all that news is blocked out, on the "capitalist" Internet.

−You will get yours, Brian, I'm sure of that!

Then I left him and went for a walk. I had no availing or dignified stuff left to say. The saurians were deep in thought and telepathy. I wished I had my companion, just then. I missed my companion walking next to me like a potted fern misses the invigorating water.

Chapter Zero

Dragon-Stars Resolution

It was Littorian himself who interrupted me early in the morning, sleeping with my two dragon-wives. I was curled up with them in the most, uh, compromising ways possible. I so didn't care at all who saw me, wow, I just didn't! This was the day after my announcement to rescue Joan.

My wives and I had a terrific, horrendously exotic session the previous night-day (yup, it lasted that long, about eight or nine hours, your local neighborhood horny teenager companion speaking, right here) and it was four in the morning when we were all satisfied, all cream-forever-more. The bed was all watery-satin and then I didn't give a shit. They'd taken care of me like a massive horny baby. All of us fell asleep immediately and had fantastic-telepathic-dreams.[3]

A wane dawn, just starting.

–I don't mean to disturb your 'bigly' creamy harvest, Larascena

---

[3] Dreaming about dragon-stars or saurians in general requires just a note. It is utterly fantastic because they can dream of you and you dream back of them! The telepathy goes into the dream as well. Loving them is like loving the air you breathe, no parallel. Jes' sayin'.

and Clareina, but could you put or pull or place or zip-up my Brian for our early morning walk? Brian's just a fountainus, gushing, sleeve-holster, for you little vixens, I presume? Or maybe it's the other way around, given Brian's dragon blood? Huh, no pressure.

–'Creamy harvest,' what's that supposed to mean, Lord Littorian? That other stuff, granted, but he put in 'creamy harvest,' hear that Lara? Your three mega-nuts be damned, too, our teenager has much larger, fatter ones via our magic, than you do, Lord Littorian! Finish waking up, there, Brian, get your generous loins off me, sheeple! We will take back our magic, now, you don't need three legs on your walk. I'm just finishing downing your elephant load with glee, mind. You'll have to build up again, shoo, shoo (and not <u>shoot</u> ((yet!)). Brian's just expecting some cash 'n' prizes gratifying his magically enhanced apparatus that's all. And by the way, Brian, you don't get my love juice for free, so come back quick! Remember, possession is nine-tenths of the law, and with anarchy, there is none!

That was Clare, winking with difficulty. Her scatological talk made me wince a bit. She was pining with life-water-superglue, making her enormous ambush of golden-silver-green eyes, as they cracked noisily, opening them. I'd gelled and semi-sealed their reptilian countenances completely with my powerful ropes, giving them both albino-looking white hair that caked and siege-creamed their orbs upon awakening. They wiped their eyes like windshields with massive claws. I, too, had my legs creaking and cracking with a plethora of saurian-life-milk as I hastily dressed in my elegant Alligatorian robe. My face had a double-stream of saurian-cream positively dripping and draining off of me, and I shook good-naturedly as a water-waded-dog when Littorian came in. This dual cream of reptilian milk hung on my whole face like a clear film, a sweet-tasting fluid, expended by two loving saurian women. I couldn't help this epic-caring-love for my saurians, no human, no teenager, ever could, I so luxuriated with them. And like any drunk human, I was inebriated with it, and after a certain point, the only thing you can do is just keep drinking-yourself-so-your-stupidly-flushed and three-sheets-to-the-wind <u>wasted</u>, you never know where your going to wash-up. I supremely loved it and slowly decamped from the saurian-soaking bed wishing to be with Littorian on this walk. I had a recent taste of being 'companion-less' on a walk. My desire for him—and them—was at breakneck-finish-line-flag-of-fabulous-notorious-*love*! I wished I could be separated out, to spend time with both my wives and my companion. With dragon magic in the air, anything can happen.

–Oh, that observation means nothing, really, my ladies. Can you have my befuddled Lloyd George, I mean, Brian Miller, ready to go? I'm glad Brian has found two saurians to love him as much as he does. I think you guys are still on your collective star-dragon honeymoon? I haven't been around vigintillions of years like Larascena has, but where does it end, two or three books later? This honeymoon, I mean?

Littorian laughed hysterically and furiously. Lara whispered a follow-up.

–That honeymoon is continuous, ending-of-nowhere, slowly. I will make him drown with my life water, you'll see, but let me get some sleep, I'm a god with a small 'g' after all of that luminous choad. My magic is indeed epic.

Larascena didn't even want to open her enormous eyes (which <u>*was*</u> possible, by-the-by, I'm not a hyper-endowed, hedonistic satyr) but batting around with Littorian's playful comments, also Larascena just murmured this:

–Uh-huh, just hurry him along, Clare, I'm doubly spent myself, he's such a glob-on. I'll have you back in my teeth-filled-mouth this afternoon, hear me Brian? And I can't be orally dislocated, though you're welcome to try your very best. Littorian, wash this satin-filled teenager off, he's just <u>soaking</u> with me.

I giggled helplessly, serpentinely getting over my wives toned, massive and overly-muscled bodies. Larascena's iron teeth were like gargantuan white ice-caps and this didn't faze me at all. They looked as healthy and vigorous as, well, dragons in their absolute prime! Their scales were just hardened silk on an ultra-warm day. I did, I must admit, bring my mouth on their dynamic abs on my way out. My tongue did a whirling rollercoaster on their bumpy, toned abdomens. My saurians laughed accordingly. Damn, I couldn't get enough of Clareina and Larascena, not ever. I did manage a response as I left for my walk with Littorian.

—Just so, my ladies, I'll wash this 'soaking' off for more later! We might be a little longer, things can wait 'til we are done. Adieu, adieu!

Of time-travel, Teresian was there for an "over-all-look-see" to make sure everything went right. Tiperia <u>could</u> do time-travel, too, but admitted she was out of practice. The 'debacle' concerning the zombie ordeal with Katrina and the Wysterian, that didn't factor into the decision to give Teresian a Chairmanship role. I guess Littorian and Tiperia were into second chances. Littorian was designated to do most of the 'time travel work.' That involved calculations that were way (way!) over my head. Thing is, Katrina would stay here, Teresian couldn't think of her going along. It would be too dangerous for her, and the zombie world adventures proved her to be right. Goodness, on that adventure, Katrina almost had her head smashed in by Teresian. The Wysterian felt so strongly about Katrina's safety that she couldn't risk her companion attending. The Russian was good natured about it, and said she'd wait at the Everglades for Teresian's return. Danillia would stay in the Everglades, too, a real relief to me. And so would my Kerok-inspired pistols. They protested with vagrant violence, that's for sure. I told them that Black World swords, knives and hatchets were appropriate, modern pistols were not, in Joan's time. They fumed and raged. I said to wait for me in the Everglades, assuring Right Two Hands and Left Two Hands that I'd be 'right' (and 'left') back!

At some point during my walk with Littorian, I waded into the waves, washing myself, and then continued our sojourn, without any water clinging to me. An Alligatorian robe was so amazing.

On our walk, I saw a random soda can, roll onto the beach, all rusted. I cringed, and I couldn't get down to business. I knew my companion saw the tin can, too, nothing got by this reptilian, not ever. I was very formal, just then.

–My liege and lord, I've got to go over some business but wish we were somewhere else. This has nothing to do with getting Stephanie Nicks to do Larascena in <u>Brian Miller Supplemental</u> as a voice-over in an animation production of <u>Brian Miller Supplemental</u>, either. It's really got nothing to do with that, although that would be my greatest joy as a writer, to have Ms. Nicks do a voice-over for Larascena.

Littorian walked over to the wave-washed soda can, picked it up, and then crushed it into the finest powder. His bicentennial muscles, casually applied, actually percolated my loins! I was very embarrassed and immediately put a saurian-mind-seal over my internal event. Meanwhile, my quirky, quaky words didn't faze him at all, and he just smiled in a toothy way. He thought I was getting some free advertising in.

–I don't think you have <u>time</u> for that maneuver. But who knows, right? Alright my companion, where do you wish to go?

–My lord, I wish to go to Anse Source d'argent, in the Seychelles, sort of northeast of Madagascar, one of those remote islands, right around there. I've only seen these islands on the Internet, though, my friend.

–Brief description?

–Uh, okay. Some beaches have a 'feeling,' an aura, well this one has an ultra-mighty-aura, and my full attention will be gripped by this place, so I can, conduct this business concerning our time-travel-trip to save Joan of Arc, my lord. The white sand through my feet, a cloudy day with a certain amount of sun just poking through those palms that are—

–Do they have rocks there?

–Rocks?

–Yes. Huge ones, it will relax me on our talk.

–I think so, my massive, giant lord, uh, yes, sure!

With that, I was seized in his six-or-seven-inch dragon-star talons, GPS was coordinated with his unimaginable mind, magic liberally employed, and we arrived in the Anse Source d'argent near Madagascar. I recovered nicely, crawling off his sleek, muscled back, looking up to the grey and white clouds. The clouds cancelled the sun for prolonged times, I figured I wouldn't be burned.

Interestingly (at least to me) Littorian's strengthened back looked 'different' from Clare and Lara's. You'd think muscle (male) = muscle (female) if you're a saurian-borne. But it wasn't that way. It's just like telling a woman writer from a male writer, just follow me in this rabbit-hole-syllogism. I can tell the difference, eight times out of ten between women writers and male writers. Maybe it's the way they use adjectives and adverbs, I don't know. Yes, I can tell. Anyway, all print journalism these days is a fat girl's dopey diary with the disintegration of paper-media in general. A saurian woman's muscles just seem gentler, more naturally flowing. Being a teenager, you have to make a conscious effort <u>not</u> to fondle a saurian woman's muscles. If you did without permission, you'd lose a hand for sure. Male saurian sinews seem more brutal and bullish. A reptilian woman is as strong as a saurian male, too, forget that at your peril. A saurian women's muscles are quite a terror if they are cross when employing them, any tragedy can result.

−No one around either, this is so excellent! Like they say about the 'Lords of the Saurians,' they can do anything…what about freedom of speech, my lord?

I bent down to the sand, and its whiteness almost made me invisible. Looking down, my companion regretted that fact.

−You can do, think and say anything you want. I've draconianly taken care of all freedom of speech issues right there! By-the-merry-way, I can improve your appearance, you know. Your wives might like it, right? Please let me try, okay? Taking on two reptilians is a lot for a human to handle.

−But not for a <u>teenage</u>-human to handle, my friend! Just remember, first chummed, first served! My appearance we can 'countenance' at the proper time, my lord. I've never been too much on how things <u>look</u>, just how they <u>perform</u>. I'm thinking that Larascena wants to get back to Beterienna, on her home-world. I think her magic has been 'building' up to the point where she can resurrect her from the distant past. That is unprecedented and it's agitating her in the extreme. I'm sure she explained everything to Clareina and maybe she is employing that Lizardanian's magic in the same direction. Beterienna means a lot to Larascena, I know. You remember Beterienna, from the Water World? Well, I know you can bleach my hair another color, and all. Maybe even renew me internally, like you cured my stroke. I've always said you are omniscient and omnipotent. Of that, later. Now, the business I have to discuss?

The green-blue waves scuttled at my bare feet and the water

rapidly dried away on the whitish sand. All was extremely-pleasant, and I prayed any can, plastic or otherwise, wouldn't appear.

Littorian was a little dismissive, but he did smile at my copious complements (if you knew what to look for; for most, he was always smiling).

–Okay, there are some limits to being a god. Only God Almighty knows no limits. Ah, yes, there are many rocks here, very good. I can stand your dragon-business now, just as long as I can entertain myself. All dragons have needs.

–Your magic will right any lives you shatter, my lord?

–Oh, yes. I'll right-everything, on leaving. Just talk very loudly during the crashing 'n' smashing, I'll listen, you'll see. And remember, there is no beach to walk on, except this one! You feel relaxed now, don't you, talking to me? I do wish to make you comfortable. Oh, and that picking up your jellyfish and throwing them out to sea and saying "It matter to that one!" is out, I've already learned that lesson from you, just-so-there!

–Alright my lord, I'll think of another lesson, anon. The sun in the sky, 72 degrees, it should be heaven, but having you in it, it's heaven-plus-+! You're so magnificent looking it's just my pleasure to be in your humble company.

–Ummm, yeah, baby, please keep up the compliments, too, as a good companion should!

–They are coming my vigorous companion. I'm glad you stuck by me, on getting saurians to come to Earth. I see now how wrong I was. It's good that, after getting Joan of Arc companioned to Anakimian that all of us just go, my royal lord.

Littorian considered.

–It's good to be wrong with a rational reason. 'Royal' lord? You flatter me. You had this rational reason, and it was <u>reasonable</u>! Always remember that, then you can reflect with added emphasis, then you can have a meaningful eucatastrophe. That's our over-all goal, you know. To understand all is to forgive all—you are at a 'synthesis' that I wanted you to come to, but definitely come to on your own. I was glad to support you in this process, but really, I didn't do anything (not being your benign antithesis, Soreidian took that role), in keeping with anarchy (or not!). Now, are we done? Well, good again. Watch this casual display of extreme-awesome power and try not to cream all over yourself, leave that for Lara and Clare!

With that, the creature went over to a rock twice the size of a double-decker-bus and lifted the whole thing, quite effortlessly. Littorian's strength, his rocketing, mountainous arms, his staggering biceps and Everest peak just had me trembling. Five feet of muscle on his arms, damn. His claws dug into the stone as he lifted it over his head-fins. Every gargantuancy my companion possessed was bulged out in a physical-fantasy-land. I immediately thought of those 'bullworker' ads of yesteryear, the muscular male (and females, too) exercising, every sinew pulsing with power. I just gaped at Littorian in absolute awe-'n'-shucks.

Ground caving in around the reptilian, all kinds of creatures were disturbed from the dragon-star-mightiness towering above them. It'd been some time that I saw my companion 'exercising' and it was drama-unforeseen. His biceps were almost as enormous as Soreidian's or the Lord of the Crocodilians, almost five feet around like a carved, sculpted mountain, creasing up in an enstrengthened titanium peak. No wonder he was deified by humans, and yet he was not a Nephilim, he was one of God's chosen angels. Well, I thought Littorian was; so, he was!

Littorian's ultra-green-porcelain-body liked that kind of weight quite nicely, but I've already said that he could take the head of Superman and chow-pulverize that cranium in his supreme claws, and stamp all over the Justice League or the Avengers until they were dust, with just a mere thought. The strength of this dragon-star could crunch anything. I just can't do any justice to his incredible massivity, he plowed over the human 'heroes' like a benign Tyrannosaurus Rex (with <u>ultimate power</u>, of course).

–Your mouth is watering a bit, but I won't tell. You're probably flattering me again, in your mind. Very well. I'm monitoring your thoughts right now, sorry to intrude. The only thing I can't crush would be the love in my heart for you, Brian. Now, then, I'm not trying to establish any parental tyranny, it's too late for that, but do you see the waves out there, crashing on the round plate of this island, right, about three miles away, my companion?

–I do my lord, it's almost on the skyline, very far away.

I wanted to encourage him, even though I'd seen him as a dragon fighting Genotdelian, the former Lord of the Crocodilians. That was an epic, supreme fight, at least what I saw of it. Thing is, I couldn't get enough of seeing him 'enstrengthened' and that over quite nothing, like now. Like a cup with no bottom, his draconian nature I wanted to bring out. Suitable blame falls on my being a teenager and wanting to see his massive power. My dual wives confronted all of my 'muscling' thoughts, my hours of wrestling around with them, and believe me my thoughts were dirty. But not 'dirty-dirty' (I know, at this young age, the difference) they were based in a love (and some lust) that knew no bounds with my saurians. It wasn't based on some concept of 'domination,' not that, I just wanted to be 'consumed' with the strength of dragons, I guess. No teenage human could ever ask for more.

Here, I just anticipated seeing Littorian's juggernaut of super-power. Quite obviously, I would die for Lara and Clare. Or Littorian. The others, well, maybe 'not so much.' These three saurians were special to me…like the Divine Trinity, maybe. No human could appreciate, really, the 'having' of my saurian wives, no human could even 'do that kinda stuff,' it was just awesome and so ineffable. They brought a 'filthy' word like 'sex' to a whole extra level, a new, extra-verified and awesome height, leaving 'filthy' far behind. As a teen, I constantly wanted it! And I'm not being a 'lazy shit' when I call it ineffable, either, so there.

Littorian threw the massive-rock-bulk and it landed (after a very high arc, staying in one piece, maybe by magic, I didn't know, didn't care) making huge destruction when it impacted.

Littorian looked satisfied, and his large eyes darted down to bagel-mouthed-me.

–Don't worry, don't worry, I'll restore all the life and decimated land occurring on our little walk.

I set my latent, very subdued homosexuality aside, as Littorian looked around for a much larger rock. I'm ashamed to admit that I had an attraction to Littorian but really, I knew it was benign. I wasn't asking to be the "second" after Tiperia, after all, not another lover. That event I'd never survive, I'd literally be turned inside out, his apparatus was that gigantic. I'd seen him making a whole-lotta-love to Tiperia, and that one incident was awesome(ness) and the Lord of the Lizardanians could fill me up to a positive explosion (in a loving way). Littorian caused me to recognize the Freud in me.

The saurian had his eye on a little mountain that was as large as the capital building in Washington, D.C. This one gigantic rock, thrown with force, pulverized the front-plate of the island and set the whole ground to quaking, it went off like a nuclear bomb. The resultant splash was incredible. All seemed effortless his breathing continued as normal. Littorian smiled in huge-gratification at the mini-apocalypse he set up.

I got down (finally) to business. He was looking for a much, much larger projectile, and my words halted him (just barely).

–Littorian of course you will have to be immunized. All of you saurians that are choosing to go back in time to save Joan of Arc, I've got the Black World weapons ready to give you the appropriate shots.

–Immunized? No, that's taken care of, my companion. Concern yourself with something other.

–Are you sure, my lord?

The Lizardanian just looked down at me, and then <u>got</u> down to my level, taking a knee. Littorian was kindly, and I felt a familiar and a gentle warmth from him, like no other. It wasn't like my reptilian wives, either. I had ineffable love for him, and my companion could see that right off. For my especial-saurians I felt such affection, a teenager's love that knew no bounds. For him, I felt life coursing through my dragon-adapted veins, and that of life itself, my love of life, it just 'pulsed' out of Littorian and through me. He was a god. He was the reason that I existed at all. Without him, I couldn't go on. I don't know if this 'companionship' exists in human life generally, but I suspect it does. It's a need to learn, and to tell what you know—I mean, the synthesis of 'what' you know. The saurians could turn your mind around all kinds of things. They wouldn't <u>force</u> you or any-such-thing. The saurians wanted you to learn <u>for yourself</u>, and, importantly, by yourself.

Littorian didn't want me to be so depended on saurians, didn't even want me to think it, but I did. No, the gods can't control you completely. The Lord of the Lizardanians could destroy whole worlds or create them—and he much, much preferred to create. My love, even though I was just a teen, was complete for my companion.

My mind focused on Genotdelian's warping me into some kind of 'disbelieve' in my companion, earlier on. To understand all is to forgive all, Tiperia and Littorian showed me a greater truth. That was probably a prime reason Genotdelian killed me. My companion ripped me out of the Grim Reaper's grasp, and that made him more than an angel to me. I'm just a teenager, I'll 'grow up' and get out of such feelings about my companion, I'm sure. But not really, with star dragon blood in my veins, already I could take on 20 or maybe 30 men, my strength growing. My life as a dragon, what would it be like? A different life? Give up on humanity as a dragon? Or can I reach out to them, as a dragon, maybe, should? Can I love being human even if I'm not?

Littorian put his hands on me, dwarfing my arms. He squeezed, but it was a loving squeeze.

—Course! You worry too much, my teenage human. I've thought of everything, as I usually do. I'm a dragon-star after all, have some genuflected deference! I'm the <u>mightiest</u> dragon-star ever, and I <u>might</u> spar with Kukulkan before we are done. We know that much about shape-shifting, everyone will be immune to everything. Of course, I'm not insulted. You care for us, I know. I wouldn't have the power needed to lift any rocks bigger than a Beetle Volkswagen, but who knows, right? I can now, and maybe that's all that matters, the future doesn't really exist? Any acting-up by any given Frenchies, I'll just clod them to near-death. I'm eons older than you, but still considered a 'young' leader of the Lizardanians. Now that the saurian war is over, I can let go of this position as Lord of the Lizardanians (but not the power, I'll keep that, ahem!). And that's only in war-time and you, Brian Miller, have single-handedly moved the great saurian community beyond war into the snuggling arms of peace! You are greater than you know. We adults tend to embarrass the children, or the teenagers. So there, my companion, be satisfied! I'll be as strong, as sinuous as any given bulking-Clydesdale, don't worry yourself about me.

—A Clydesdale is a draft horse and can move 8,000 pounds, my lord. I read that on the Internet(s).

—Just that, 8,000 pounds, my companion? Well, to get Joan of Arc lifted from that lil' French stake, we must all be prepared to sacrifice. I have my girlfriend Tiperia handling it. Oh, the pains of being Lord of the Lizardanians! Can I stand the strain a moment longer? Your familiar with Star Trek, right?

–Gosh, which one, which franchise, that's like saying Star Wars, I just hope I get my acknowledgements right, writers hate to be plagiarized, my lord?

–Plagiarized, here? We are on our own frontier dealing with dragon-stars, damn. I'm into specifics! Have you seen _The City on the Edge of Forever_?

–Written by Harlan Ellison? I like to give credit where credit is due, my gracious lord!

–Good, good. If we change one thing in time, if one person dies, who knows what changes that will make throughout time. Time has to resume the shape that it has, or maybe even all saurians might never come to Earth. Whether that is for good or ill, you decide.

–I get you Lord Littorian. We'll be careful.

–Both of us will have to be careful, my friend, and we don't like going back or forward in time you understand?

–That wasn't the only <u>time</u> they dealt with <u>Time</u>, my lord. In _The Naked Time_, written by John D. F. Black, when the ship went into a time-warp, going backwards in time and—

Littorian waved his hand and laughed at himself, myriad teeth raging in the sunlight. Then, he talked of the Supreme God of Everything, the spy systems of the world, the British people, the books I'd read, my articles, my 'quiet revolution,' my utmost thoughts (and his) about everything and every-when, living forever as a dragon, the fact that my Dad walked out on my Mom before (and, ergo, why I was a good companion that-a-way), my family and their 'disposition' (which was cool, he'd take care of them, *par excellence*), and he talked about strings, sealing-wax, and other fancy stuff!

We had a roaring fire that night, (and maybe another night,

I can't remember; talking to him was so fascinating, I could do it forever) talking and talking and thinking and thinking! We discussed things through telepathy and verbally.

Littorian 'righted' things at the end of our little couple-of-days-walk. All life was restored, all was fine. After, I was all set on finding Joan of Arc and that everything would go right given that I was amongst gods. How appreciably wrong I was about everything going right!

Chapter One

Exquisite 15th Century-Banner

I reflected on Anakimian's 'review' of that friendless child's life. She was only 19 years old--and yet 50 or 60 books were consumed by the reptilian, thousands of hours on her life rapaciously eaten by the great Alligatorian eyes, and (yet!) <u>still</u> he wasn't satisfied. He saw all the many movies on that helpless girl. Some movies weren't as well-constructed as others, like <u>The Messenger</u> (which was a fine movie for 'todays standerts'). It was like taking H.P. Lovecraft's 1931 notes on the <u>Mountains of Madness</u>, and being able to interpret every and all lines of scribble therein!

Anakimian's been anywhere and everywhere on YouTube. com and had completely "draconically" ravaged the whole Web for data on Joan of Arc. It was, I must admit, inspiring to see a dragon-star researching his companion-for-life like this. All of this only 'wetted' the young Alligatorians insatiable appetite. I couldn't believe how <u>fast</u> he could read French, English and even medieval French! For instance, if the Alligatorian saw a parchment on any 'screen' (like on Youtube.com, for instance) he could read it and <u>know</u> what it said, all within a moment of looking at it. Just amazing creatures, really.

Anakimian reproached me severely, saying that he had to

rescue this angelic child from the flame, and did I have even more information on that peasant girl? At wit's end (and over it) I just said 'Hey, man, wait until we get with this girl, damn, then you'll see!' He wasn't even my companion, I was just his substitute-companion, and he was driving me berserk.[4] Anakimian's tolerance for me was exceeding his 'tolerance line' and I knew how powerful he was. Still, I didn't go to my wives or Littorian, I thought I could handle it. I couldn't wait for my shape-shifted Alligatorian-friend to companion with that Child of the Sun and let loose of him entirely. Two companions, too much!

The Alligatorian already knew everything about France in the 13th, 14th and 15th centuries, still wanted more and was put-out by my 'tardy' response. He knew the history of that natural-comrade-of-the-bird, and then he brazenly said he wanted to learn about Oliver Cromwell and the Republic in England! My Black

---

[4] Anakimian read books by Twain, Shaw, Gordon, West, Butler, Warner, Wilkinson, Pernoud, Devries, Seward, Wilson-Smith, Williams, Clin, Bartlett, Anouilh, Schiller, Endore, and more than this. I noticed Anakimian had some books within his easy reach. He keyed on Joan of Arc: In Her Own Words, by William Trask, and Joan of Arc: Fact, Legend and Literature by Wilfred T. Jewkes and Jerome B. Landfield. The latter was a college book, I saw that immediately. Then he had a Horizon Magazine book, on Joan of Arc, too. On French plays concerning Joan, he was a mega-master—he knew every word, for instance, of L'Alouette by de Jean Anouilh. Anakimian was all set on a 'delivery technique' to get on Joan's good side I figured. The saurian already knew she was 'troubled,' and a lil' bit crazy! The Alligatorian still wanted more, more on the Maid! He just 'took over' ¾ of my available desk-space. Anakimian just moved into my office-entire, really, and thank God it was big enough to have one ravaging, de-lux-with-a-mission saurian. Anakimian asked Littorian about what it was like having a companion. Littorian just said find out for yourself!

World knives, my ad-hoc librarians, were at sixes and sevens to keep up with his supreme demand for books (and everything else of any kind of literature, electronic or otherwise) on Jehanette and on Cromwell!

Incidentally, Anakimian corrected me on 'man'—'dragon-star or 'star-dragon' he'd accept but me 'smacking' him on 'man' was going down a notch, almost calling him a 'simian.' I didn't want to feel his claws across my face, and definitely apologized, as a good substitute-companion should. If you call a saurian a 'worm' or something atrocious, that's just plain suicide.

As of the fate of Jing and her 'diplomatic' gestures with Tercharian, the recollection was wormwood. She thought it to me, and I just cringed at that memory she retained about getting burned up by Tercharian. That 'set' of thoughts really disturbed me, the saurian power was so great. The foil is the Black World sword, which she casually left behind her! Damn, that was dumb. I thought we made this clear during training: Never be without a Black Sword when dealing outside your companion. If your companion 'turned against you,' well, then, you'd have no reason to live. This is just my own perspective from being a reptilian companion, without them, for me, there is no life. I'm not trying to spread this idea around, I'm just telling you how it is for me, personally. Before the Twins of Triton adventure, my life was, well, just a life. It was something I wanted to live for, my life with Littorian. And my saurian wives, also. It was as near to Heaven as I'm going to get.

Tercharian sure met his fate with the new-Lord of the Crocodilians. However, the very thought of such an incineration for humans could give you 'shell shock' that's for sure. They are so awesomely powerful, that they can deal with problems only draconianly, and in an absolute manner. You have to be doubly careful when you 'give' problems to saurians, because they will double-down and 'really' solve them but for good. Their 'kind' of 'good' isn't really human's kind of 'good' if you know what I mean. They can be reasonable, that's sure, and this is where diplomacy comes in. Alligatorians and Lizardanians can 'make' a flame, but it's only by magic. Not as hot as any sun, like the Crocodilians can. The Crocs were masters at fire, be sure to genuflect there. Well, enough.

It's true that any saurian can efface anything and everything with one touch from their talented, reptilian claws. They could cleave through anything, could cut a diamond in half, yet on human skin those same-self claws (female claws, I'm talking about) were heavenly, divine and just so ultra-absolute, it shakes me even to tell just a little bit, with semi-adequate words! Love is sweaty-sticky, and as a teen, I emotively love it, it was so much better than any kind of drug!

Just in thinking about it, a teenager is completely aroused about any saurian-full-grown-female they see. I couldn't help myself, and no honest human could! They are just fantastic looking. Seeing the muscles on a saurian, damn, you know they can 'work' and beyond description, too. Balderdash-the-doubt, the saurians are spectacular, especially the 'fairer sex.' That seems misogynous today, with our political correctness, I mean it sincerely. Besides, 'political' means nothing to a 'dutiful' saurian anarchist. Duh.

Of course, I didn't lecture Anakimian on the facts dealing with Joan. He absolutely recalled anything and everything on the Maid, rapaciously so. You can't trust the French or English when it comes to religion, I told him. Anakimian just scoffed. That's a sign that you're going too far on your coaching. If it was a Crocodilian, you'd see a puff of smoke from their nostrils. And where there is smoke...

Joan wasn't an 'ordinary' peasant, either. Her Dad was an official, of sorts, in his town, sort of a mayor. In 15th century France, lots of girls ran around "hearing voices" and death was so close, you can almost see it. I mean, people only lived to around 30 or so. Rare the elderly human going beyond that limit. You look at entertainers, for instance, and become enthralled by them; thing is, that's not the way they really are in real life. Sometimes they are positively sinister, and that's a downer to folks interested in 'worshipping' someone.

On the instant of time-travel, Littorian taking the lead, and closing his masterful silver-golden eyes, I felt a rocking of sorts. I saw Danillia and Katrina just eyeing each other. Danillia was smiling, and, at the time, I didn't know why. All the dragons and companions were together, Kerok waving us off, and time 'performed' backward. His companion, Nausicaä Lee, stood by him. And "Performed" is the right word, everything going into reverse in a funny way. It wasn't violent, but all of us were somewhat 'jolted' back and forth, just a little.

After arriving back, at the village just before Joan's capture at the town of Compiegne, we added to our 'cartel.' We hired Esteban Diaz Paredes, a master and a town lord of sorts. Under Esteban were five people, following the master's orders exactly. All of them were a right-and-trite augmentation of our courtly crew of Burgundian-'wanna-bes.' Littorian, in shape-shifted form, paid him handsomely for 'seeing' us all around. Esteban himself carried our Burgundian standard on horseback. Everyone's slightest need was more-than-satisfied by Diaz Paredes' folks, and that right away. All the shape-shifters were satisfied.

So, all of us were at the hill top, overlooking the bog. It did seem like a dream to me. I couldn't believe how well our nobility-and-clergy-shape-shifted so easily into the <u>reality</u> before us. Joan's capture was taking place. It wasn't what we expected, however.

Before me, a sight to see. The thrill of being transported back to ancient France, in the year 1430 wasn't the half of it. I looked on at Joan of Arc, doing a silent Edvard Munch 'Scream' imitation. Joan was in a little bog outside a grey castle in Compiegne.

–You don't want some of *this*! You filthy, sniveling, scat-eating, God-have-mercy on your (offal) souls, vile Burgundian *villains*! I'll give you some of this vial nigglet! I'll toss you sniveling, toadfish, dirt bags!

The awkward way this teen-angel spoke was remarkable. Her French, said in a shrill, higher-war cry, was sort of indiscernible (even to her dying Armagnac followers around her). It was like listening to a British person *today* talking to an Englishman from Shakespeare's time. Some words went totally 'over' all of us, even Anakimian with all he knew about Joan's time, placed his hand on his shape-shifted chin, thinking deeply. Scratching my head, I was standing aghast over Joan's small band of patriotic followers, overlooking the bog, wringing my hands.

Of-a-sudden, two arrows whizzed, and Joan of Arc's horse was struck in the upper neck. Forlorn, I wanted to leap to the Maid of Vancouleurs' aid, not caring about the deadly arrows. I knew of two occasions were a bolt and an arrow wounded Joan, and she'd survived. The lance in the girl's mailed hands didn't kill anyone, I noticed. Indeed, during her trial, she said she didn't kill anyone at all, not in her many campaigns as general to King Charles VII.

I saw her brilliant horse go down, blood squirted and whizzed around the two punctures. Then the blood splayed in ropes on Joan of Arc's upper torso. Yes, the Maid was hurtled down; but <u>then</u> she got started. Her shawl was pulled back, by a foot-soldier-ruffian-scamp. I hated this shit-baggy-pants-right-off, and only Larascena's shape-shifted hand, held me back from running down the hill to give him the *what-for*! Her grip was not so strong that I couldn't break it, however. I was used to her reptilian mightiness, but when shape-shifted, it was just a human hand. She was admittedly strong, though. My shape-shifted wife was right in holding me back. The Alligatorian warlord smiled at me, and said it would be alright, and that we would save the Chosen servant. So, I just did nothing, very reluctantly, and then she took her hand off of my shoulder.

Joan's wounded horse splayed, prancing awkwardly in the mud, it was all too much for me, right then. Shock and horror engulfed The Maid, in front of the castle. She loved her horse, really depended on it in the extreme, and felt his pain as though it was happening to her.

That Embodied prodigy's prized horse was almost everything to the Maid, and how easily killed was he. The horse took three Burgundians with him, however, just Percheron-stamped them into the mud. Then the horse went down, dead before he hit the ground. I checked myself, wanting to help. Things had to 'play out' in the historical way. Her cry was all that could be heard; the bridge was gone, upraised into the castle. No retreat.

Then, I saw something mesmerizing. This slender statue of the somber human was using the Asian Arts; she was great at Karate and Kung-fu! Joan was pulled down, but she took advantage, did a summersault and had both feet into the surprised chests of her two foremost assaulters. Right then, I heard a song in my mind from that movie the Matrix, Trinity going to town, running off the walls, I think the song is called Spybreak, by the Propellerheads. I know, but listen to the music, then you'll realized the majesty of that exciting moment, too.

The Burgundians flew back and were pasted right in the mud with a slash-n-splash, the kick from Joan was so violent. Jing and Sheeta, standing silently with their shape-shifted companions, were completely fascinated at the Herald of God's awesome kick. Casting her banner aside, she set on her assailants as a cat with so many nuisance-mice. In spite of the Burgundian captain's orders, an arrow <u>did</u> shoot towards Jehanne la Pucelle and she just barely managed to dodge it! Incredibly, it ran through her bob haircut and got stuck in the eye of one of her assailants, coming out the back of his head. The captain was beside himself.

–Don't kill her, you fool! Goddamn your eyes, surrender those arrows, ho! How many more men have we? All of you go at once, without weapons you shit bags, just wrestle her down!

That's not what shocked me the most. My shape-shifted comrades were at sixes-and-sevens at Joan's raucous antics, too.

Littorian was flummoxed at Joan's war-cry.

–Maybe, in this time, I should modify my quote *To understand all, is to forgive all,* with *Ab uno disce omnes* (from <u>one</u> we learn to know all)?

Equally bagel-mouthed at this Trumpian-logic, I responded smartly and churned out just-this:

–Yes, my lord, maybe that would be best. I just hope I'm that <u>one</u>. That is, the one who learns.

–You might be that one, yes. Anakimian will have his mighty, flowery claws so full of Joan of Arc. Pre-pun intended. I wonder if he can handle it? Her father was sort of a mayor in his little town, she also might be high-flown?

–Could be, we'll see, if history is allowed to play out, my lord.

Then, something happened. Littorian turned to the East getting a curious look. The shape-shifted countenance was troubled.

–It just couldn't be…

Chapter Two
The Maid's Burgundian Adventure

J ing Chang was thinking about The Middle Kingdom, she told me, and about the exciting moves and motions of Joan of Arc. She was totally fascinated by the Kung-Fu and Jiu Jistu displayed by the Maid. Similarly, Sheeta Miyazaki resolved:

–Oh, this girl must be saved. She's a dangerous saint! Jing and I could teach her still more, and with dragon blood in that modest teen, she'd be so fast, she could avoid arrow strikes and sword blows. Anakimian, you must, must save her!

On the top of the hillock, only the company of companions and shape-shifters heard Sheeta. Anakimian wanted to preserve the girl, but not until 30 May 1431—then and only then. The saurians were impressed too: It was ten minutes of battle before the girl was subdued. Clareina and Larascena looked down with unhappiness at seeing her caught.

Killed, all of her comrades in chains or massacred, this funereally black teen saw there was no way out. Anakimian watched her. Eventually, with 20 more men applied, they got Joan subdued, tying her with stout ropes.

Her followers were either cut-up, taken prisoner, or ran off. Those that fell trying to defend their female general, I nearly cried over. It was atrocious for me, the whole scene.

At the end, there were three horse-stomped-on men, seven more with Joan of Arc's beatings (and I didn't hear anyone say the Maid put up so terrific a fight in the trial transcripts). The amount of blood and fleshy-offal made the air about her waxen face thick, and we all got a few whiffs on the hillock. The captain and three of his minions flew up on horses to meet us with their joyous news. The head-of-the-hunt had his banner with him. He stopped his horse, I couldn't see anything because of the dust, even though he was going uphill. The captain, overjoyed, looked at our Burgundian banner, and nodded appreciably.

–We've got Joan, ho, did you see?

Littorian was first with a response.

–It cost you a lot, my man, apprehending that innocent creature? Everything is flammable, even her! You did manage a good pile-on, though, a marvelous captain that you are, what, uh, 'ho'?

At this affront, the Burgundian had issue. Littorian just blew it all off, but that 'off-blowing' offended the knight all the more. A little tuff was beginning. Littorian was doing diplomacy and our group was so 'thunderstruck' at seeing Joan's capture, he rightly headed our group by default. He did have a lot of experience. I didn't know we would see the same captain-knight at court, later. Littorian and the captain had more words, some a little rocky.

I had my Black World weapons on me and no one thought it out of favor at all letting Littorian sport with the Burgundian captain. I had one of my knives in hand, just in case, and I squeezed the handle around.

I'm here for you, Brian, don't you worry.

Please don't do anything, we can't upset history!

But here, everyone has knives, hatchets, swords, I'm in pretty good company, even though I'm black. No racism here, I see? No one's given me notice at all.

The telepathy of the Black weapon reassured me. At least I had this resource.

Littorian introduced all of us all to the captain-knight in our Burgundian group, included all the helpers. I was a page and attached to Littorian. A very minor page. My given roll with a (fountain) pen, I was used to it.

I don't have time to think about what saurians shape-shifted into what Frenchies. The English didn't see anyone shape-shifting into <u>their</u> ranks. It was a unique process to be sure.

After her journeys, probably to show-off the fact that Joan of Arc had been captured, we arrived at Rouen. I had other problems, things I didn't expect, and that required all my attention and then some(more). I know certain people constituted the 'real-deal,' and definitely weren't shape-shifted into, like the Earl of Warwick, that shit-eating English earl; John de Stogumber, the heaven-pleading chaplain (he regretted his attacks on the Maid, but only God forgives, right?). Pierre Cauchon, a foreskin-shill for the English (I thought he was the lowest human I'd ever met); Jean D'Estivet, the prosecutor (a lawyer's lawyer would sent this guy to Hell, that punk actually spit on her!); Jean Beaupere (some-kinda-poo-bag-par-excellence); and those sorta-similar people, most of the 'church' people were hostile to Joan but not, indeed, all.

The shape-shifters were people like Courcelles (I don't know who of the saurians was that guy, sorry); Brother Martin Ladvenu (again, I don't know which saurian 'pretended' to be that fellow); the vice-inquisitor, Jean Le Maistre, (who diffidently refused to cooperate with the English until his very life was threatened); Guillaume Manchon (an honest man) and the chief notary; Thomas de Courcelles (one of the University of Paris gentleman); Jean Lefevre (who protested the Maid answering whether she was in a State of Grace or not); and the Duchess of Bedford (who oversaw the 'strip search' of La Pucelle and found her to be a virgin) and Joan had many minions, all women—some of these I'm sure were saurians. History had to transpire. The saurians would see to it. And there was Maitre Nicolas Loyseleur, someone on Cauchon's side, he was kinda a double-agent; Maitre Jean Lohier, Norman Clerk and some others. There was no counsel, as such, for the girl, to answer the Church Masters and Doctors and our noxious Shit-talkers (and these latter were legion).

We all knew what the results would be anyway.

Joan of Arc confessed that everything had been a ruse, and then she defied all over that little section in Deuteronomy, saying that she sported men's clothes as not to get raped. She was turned over to the secular arm of the church. Anakimian would companion with Joan and watched the English guards close but wasn't with her towards the end. Joan looked for Anakimian, he played a minor Brother-of-the-church, but he was a dragon on that final day. Anakimian wouldn't let the flame find Joan of Arc.

Oh, there were others, of course, The Dauphin (the political Charles VII, sorta a nasty little thing); the Archbishop of Rheims (politician-writ-large); Monseigneur de la Tremouille (he resented Joan when she got in control of Armagnac forces); Gilles de Rais, one loyal to Joan but he had other (perhaps, later) interests. Dunois (The Bastard), young, dumb, fulla-ahem, and not convinced that the Maid should be saved. Yes, I marked that down. The times (1431) make the (wo)men. That was the whole thing. Damn skippy, if I could have <u>seen</u> what was coming, I wouldn't have suggested any of this adventure!

Chapter Three

An Atrocious Teenage Saint

Since Joan was captured (and that for a year!), I had nothing to do. I had my wives to 'visit' and that twice or three times a day, which I really liked. Even so, I had no 'marriage vows,' on them at all so if they wanted to 'sleep around' on me, that'd be fine. I didn't ask them anyway, about their 'affairs and liaisons' because that wouldn't be 'keeping' with anarchy. Still, I'll ask them first if I wanted to sleep around, I have no secrets, and that's just how I roll (I hate that expression, same as 'genre'—yuck—a shitty French word).

So, I walked around Rouen, France, thinking, lost in my own personal revere. Jes' kicking down the cobblestones (literally), looking for fun and feelin' groovy (an ode to Simon and Garfunkel, ding-ding!). The winter was just fading away, it was February 1431—May 30 followed hard-upon, and I looked forward to getting Joan away. Well, I wouldn't be doing it, she was in 'saurian control' and, really, 'Tiperia-control'. In this, I was comfortable. I never would have guessed what was coming.

Of the words and events of Joan of Arc, all of that is written, and that's a good thing, too. It was written, <u>again</u> after our time-travel adventure, very lucky for us. I took comfort in our collective situation and every word came off as though no one had shape-shifted at all. The shape-shifted 'people' had to 'fit' right into the scenario of the trial of Joan of Arc. Anakimian would keep watch over Joan—until the end. She'd be safe enough with that saurian's care. I had to remember that she had been wounded at least twice, and that she was a general. These were, of course, the end of the Dark Ages and Joan is a witch and all. I laughed at such a thing. If she were a witch, then why wouldn't she leave, why stick around at all? Things were hard on her, but it'd be all over soon. The rest of the royal companionship had it relatively good.

(Un)ironically, Joan was ultimately condemned on being a cross-dresser (dressing in men's clothes, which according to Deuteronomy 22:5, women can't wear men's clothing because it would be an abomination to Yahweh, that is, your ('our') God. The Lizardanians were calm with this; the Alligatorians thought it laughable; and the Crocodilians were indifferent. Although I didn't have extensive talks to the Crocodilians on religion, I just thought of them as agnostic, and left it at that.

Ironical to me, that the saurians were acting out as men and women, not caring about if they were 'regularly' men or women when dragon-stars! In a way, they were ignoring Deuteronomy, too. You talk about your 'cross-dressing' the saurians made, wow! Frankly, I couldn't tell males and females if and when they were shape-shifted, but I knew who they really were anyway. I ran all this by Lara and Clare and they kinda blew-me-off (well, not literally). I had just been thinking romantically about Clare (but her fine, awesome muscled tail was right in front of me, how can any male teenager get enough of that sexy-back?), and since I was sitting down, my hand joined my face in a delightful little grin, eyes glanced and glazed, a hunger on my lips that only resides with a teen male.

On a cloudy day in June, rain coming as a grey veil, the Maid tried to escape from the tower in Beauvoir. Joan was clinging to a bed sheet and fell about 30 feet banging her head.

Anakimian saw this and so wanted to help the Herald of God, even to break her fall in shape-shifted form. He had to come see her chance to flee, knowing of it through his studies. He couldn't alleviant her pain, that he knew would arrive. The shape-shifted Alligatorian didn't move, and the rough guards arrived to bring the semi-conscious girl back to her cell. This was the mid-point in her capture. Maybe Anakimian was suffering from not being a dragon-star just now. That's another reason not to travel in time; anything you do could have dire consequences. Anakimian walked back, rapidly thinking and completely morose.

In the royal court, a funny scene was developing. Funny and tragic. There was Jeannette's trial and it's been recorded in history. The shape-shifters didn't do 'thing-one' to change any of it. Joan's capture and trial were fascinating but that's not a quarter of it. Yeah, she was crazy, but anyone is after five minutes of conversation with them (or they become so, just give them a little more time!).

As to the months and months of her trial, well, you can read all that Anakimian did over those 19 years, all the books and everything written on her story. Joan had a collection of 'churchy' problems, stuff I wasn't too big on, like how many angels can you stack on a pin head, stuff like that, boring little notions. The English wanted her dead, and that quickly. If the English had captured her and not the Burgundians, she'd have been sliced up and that'd be the end of it. Also, the influence Joan-the-future-martyr had over the French people had to be addressed. They needed to make her a "Mid-Evil" witch to 'satisfy' the public, excommunicate her, then kill the witch they'd created.

I'd had a couple of interviews with Joan when things were

going against her, in her prison. I couldn't go in alone, but with a group. I couldn't even ask her direct questions, not even when she was born! I think it was on the 6th of January 1412. I knew she was a teenager, and not just from the way she beat-up the Burgundians capturing her. That fascinated Jing and Sheeta.

As for 'daily life,' the saurian shape-shifters nestled right in. Anyway, her food and surroundings were pretty poor. The 100 years' war (it lasted longer than that) was the backdrop of (this) conflict between the French and the English. Further, no one knows of the terrific fight she waged against being caught! I saw that first hand and was amazed at all the miracles Jeannette manufactured. You see, people, maybe minor church officials, might become suspicious of me. They should have seen me with Death Incarnate, and that gives me shivers-unparalleled.

Chapter Four

Littorian's Knightly Challenge

The confrontation between the Lord of the Lizardanians and the Burgundian knight proceeded after a light rain fall, towards the afternoon.

Littorian's diplomacy failed when dealing with this thug, and the silly guy wouldn't leave Littorian alone! Somehow, Littorian impugned the knight's 'honor'! There was only one way to deal with that, just immerging from the Dark Ages like France was.

–Come sir, come! All day I haven't! And you, page, how stupid I think most pages are. Be you off, fool, sick to death of you I am!

The brigand was meaning _me_! I knew enough French to realize this. Littorian pushed me back, in a well-meaning way, shooing me towards the other shape-shifters. We all left immediately for the field outside the castle. There was no planning now, and I didn't think their needed to be. This captain-knight was a shit-and-a-half, and needed to be 'put-down' goodly, and big league, too! Littorian through the gullet back at the captain.

–I'll follow on, let's begin! No need to be diplomatic here.

–Not yet, you need a knightly sword, and a dagger, put that Black sword down, if you please! Come here and choose one!

I didn't know what was going on. Momently, the Burgundian

knight came right up to me. I instantly could feel my plans falling apart, bit by bit. Or, as Lara would say, bite by bite!

–Do you know what I favor, Master Page?

The French guy was in shiny armor.

–What's that, Nantucket?

–Fresh kill. This one has <u>that</u> all over him. After I'm finished with his swoony, scrawny ass, page-ums, I'll come back and make your butt into a baguette, just give me half a minute. I don't know what 'Nantucket' means, but I'm sure it's at my expense.

He turned back to his side of the field. His Burgundian and English friends, all clapped for the knight, with 'Bravo, captain!'.

–Is that captain going to deprive you of your own Black Sword from the Black World? That's an outrage, my lord you can't stand for this!

Littorian looked at the knight and his many hangers-on, and just shrugged.

–It seems so, Brian. Just stand aside. Clareina, Larascena. Don't let Brian interfere, keep him here, please. You too, Teresian, would you?

–Ah, you'll show that guy a thing or two. Please don't kill him, but with your saurian swordsmanship, I know it will be hard.

–Well, I'm afraid my swordsmanship went out the window with my Black Sword and other weapons being held by my ladies. I don't know how to use these kinds of weapons, not without their Black World help. I'm great in saurian form with their assistance; and an atrocious novice without them. I don't know the techniques of these weapons at all, don't know the first thing about them. My Black sword didn't transfer anything about 'how' to use a sword. I'm in some kind of a pickle here.

At first, I didn't believe Littorian, and just blankly stared at him. The fact that he used the French word 'pickle' here had me at sixes-and-sevens. Of a sound-sudden, I noticed Teresian took a position behind me! I had the three shape-shifters at 33-degree angles to me. I didn't notice it then. My Black World weapons, however, were under the same strictures that the other saurians' suffered! If you don't know what to do, it doesn't manner how 'simple' it is, and I didn't see the plan.

Of course, this was medieval times, I had my place as a minor page. But I was companioned to this saurian. He was shape-shifted, but that had no impact on me. Indeed, no matter who my companion shape-shifted into, I could still recognize him. Maybe it was in the eyes. Probably that. In a way, I saw his very soul and spirit. It's like looking at an angel; when you do see an angel, you know it.

Events happened quickly. The knight was surprised at his sudden victory after only five minutes past! He wasn't thrusting as hard as he might against Littorian. That was the only thing saving Littorian from being split open on this field, like two hay bales. Things were quickly going wrong for Littorian. He had two grievous wounds, and all living humans could not survive a third. I thrust forward.

—Save him, save him!

The trio then had their hands on me, didn't care a thing about my screaming and crying. The decisive bloody blow from the Burgundian sword fell down on my companion! I thought I could break everyone's grip, but I didn't want to hurt them. That diffidence delayed me, in those few seconds. I could break out, but seconds counted, then! At the length of reading these very words, I was just too late.

I noticed that all the female shape-shifters had their heads lowered, but arms fully stretched out, holding me firmly.

As a miracle-for-the-time, Tiperia came rushing in, and deflected the Burgundian stroke with her own Black World sword at the last moment, creating such a clang! The pressure on my shoulders was instantly relieved. Teresian, Larascena and Clareina then back away.

Littorian's lover had saved him. And Tiperia gave the antagonist such a kung-fu kick that landed him (with a severely dented breast-plate) near his shocked buddies. Surprised I was!

After, the English and Burgundian friends rushed over, and got a similar beating from Tiperia. She left them all bruised but alive.

–This match is over. You have won, my dented Burgundian knight. You have won your silly honor back. Now, to quote <u>A Secret Garden</u>, 'all depart'!

After the fight, I had Littorian in a little hospital, outside of Rouen. This place was for the plague, so I was a bit leery. The doctors were thinking of treatments for Littorian.

–Don't bleed him, hear? That's Dark Ages stuff.

–Dark ages, where do you think you are, page?

–Be out of here with that quackery, with that self-same piffle! I'll take care of him, just bring me a tub of water!

Tiperia was stationed at the door. She looked only once at the exhausted shape-shifter that was her lover. Then, Tiperia took her Black World Sword, stuck it in the ground with severity, winked at me, and had a seat on the bench against the front of the building. She waited. I shut the door and sat down on a stool.

–I remember you before, on that island, yes, my otiose, vain companion?

I had him all patched-up, we relied on time to make him better. And it would take good-ole-fashion-human-time to improve the shape-shifted Littorian.

–Of Madagascar, right, my human friend? Ouch, this hurts, be careful adjusting me.

I dabbed his face with my parchment-cloth. He was being really human now. His fever broke a short time ago, so I figured he was out of danger.

–You looked so strong, so mighty, you know, hurtling those boulders around, like a god, if you please, just really a super-saurian.

–And now?

I winced.

–Not so much. I'm overusing that phrase, and I'm sorry, my gracious lord, I'm also sorry for giving you unsolicited advice.

–It's okay. I deserve worse (than an over-used phrase). Dumbness has no bounds, 'least I'm good at something. Damn, that was so stupid taking on that knight.

–Why did you tell those saurians not to interfere, geez, your own Black World weapons, designed to protect you, my lord?

–Honor, really.

–Honor! That smacks anarchy in the face until it comes off completely!

–Not honor for the saurians, not that. Honor for my lover, I knew she'd be there.

–For Tiperia?

–Sure. Doesn't she 'wait on me' now, outside this building, kind of like in that film <u>The Shadowless Sword</u>, right? She protected the prince, remember?

–I remember the film, I thought you'd like it. I figured you were in sound-saurian-sleep, then, you always fall asleep when I'm showing you movies.

–Didn't fall asleep noticing that.

–She is guarding you now?

—She doesn't want to see even my shape-shifted self getting into trouble.

—You're lucky, my lord.

—Don't think your wives are watching out for you that way? They are.

—Sleep now. I'm standing by you, as a good companion should.

Chapter Five

My Chess Game with Death Incarnate

One month before 'the end' with Joan, I was walking side-roads of Rouen. There wasn't much for me to do, lest pining over that little angel's inevitable disposition. Littorian was recovering nicely. Meanwhile, the shape-shifters would see that things didn't go too badly for the Maid. I knew her imprisoned life to be hard, though, following the history right along.

In Rouen, the Black Plague was somewhat declining, but you could still see doctors, dressed for the Black Death and other human troubles (which were legion). They were hooded, and had an elongated, black beak of incense and myrrh, making them appear as a stork rather than as any regular physician. The guy I was looking at was as thin as a stork, too, looking for fish and not finding any.

I recognized two of them talking at the end of an alleyway and I stopped to look at them, just absently. They were crazily dressed all in black, but other folks just walked right by them without a second thought. The taller one looked my way.

My mind and my very heart was filled with forlornness right then. The doctor put a hand up to his talkative shorter companion. The other physician abruptly left, almost clicked, like something mechanical and automated, and did an about-face, marching off like a drummer-toy.

Then, I knew.

Oh, the 'stupidity' of my plan smote me entirely. All of it, my plan just a medley of human stupefaction. I thought that bringing Joan of Arc back would be safe enough, we <u>did</u> need a leader of the 30 companions. I didn't know that I had endangered all my saurians, just by this one suggestion. They were shape-shifted and could be killed here in the past.

It was Death Incarnate!

My companions, were they going to be his victims, too? All of them, Larascena, Clareina, Littorian, Anakimian, all saurians coming back with us, they were shape-shifted and the 'rules' of being human applied. They were human now, subject to human 'rules.' Oh, rules! They cried in the face of anarchism, and it was rudely slapped back across the (all-too-human) pate! The saurians couldn't 'change back,' unless time-travel was involved, or would <u>shortly be</u> involved. Tiperia, did she have her power? All my thoughts were in a jumble, like clothes rumbling around in an over-stuff dryer.

Of course, I couldn't telepathically think to any of them with this problem. I'd have to deal with it myself. I covered my conscious mind. I feigned an image of my stroke and overlaid that on my very brain. Hopefully, Death Incarnate would see that <u>reflection</u> of the past, and not investigate it further. That was my (only) hope.

Death Incarnate couldn't know that I'd fully recovered from my stroke and that at the benign hand of the Lord of the Lizardanians. Did Death Incarnate have such knowledge? I hoped not. I also had a power in me making my strength thirty times any man, thanks to dragon-blood. I had that kind of strength bubbling within me. That wouldn't count against Death Incarnate, but it was an advantage. An advantage how? First, I was really fit, and my mind hyper-active. I feigned my stroke and the weak nature that it caused, I even got back my little limp as I walked up to Him. I had a plan, and it was desperate, just like me, half the time.

The Black Doctor came up to me, his cape held by this left, boney hand.

–Time to go, Brian, right? Men lead quietly desperate lives—but your time is over.

–Correction, I'm a teenager. My body is ready, my lord Death Incarnate, but my soul is not.

–Your contriteness underwhelms me. I give no respite, soul or otherwise, you ought to know that by now, there are no dragons to save you. I've seen many suns as cold as ice, souls, like yours, all emptied out in human death stares as I took them. It's so glorious.

I ignored what I couldn't understand.

–You're a great, fantastic chess player, isn't that right, my dark lord?

–You know that how?

–Pictures, films, books, in the Western World communication rules all, my dark lord?

–Chess is my one weakness.

–Thing is, you're not as skilled as me.

–What?!

–My dark lord, I mean, but my <u>bet</u> remains, forever-more.

–Nice to have respect when Death Incarnate is near?

–I <u>do</u> have it, but you can't win at chess against me.
Death Incarnate sighed.

–Obviously you've seen _The Seventh Seal_, right Brian?

–That's got nothing to do with this, my dark lord.

–I can't lose against you Brian, I have foreseen it!

–Then you'll do me the honor of playing me?

–And then, I will take you. You played a good game to get so far, but now your time is up.

–This game could last a month I have some affairs to attend to.

–Like your saurians watching Joan of Arc die, you mean?

I blinked but kept right on with the beginning lie. Hey, that was convenient, Death Incarnate just thought we were there to <u>watch</u>, not make a <u>girl-switch</u>! He had no right idea of the future, he only knew His role in it! I had to be very careful now.

–Yes, well, as you no doubt know, you can't upset history at all, no telling where things might go after a fatal event, no matter how small. That's why we are just here to watch, it's good for the historical perspective I'm trying to teach the saurians. Then we'll leave the Earth. This is just so Rachel and Jason can say "So there!" when we go, they are such rascals. Human beings make the Earth so corrupt, in past and future, any fool can see this. So, it's a 'yes' on my tending to affairs, right my dark lord?

I didn't want to stretch the lie too far.

–Affairs? Isn't that the cat's tit, young human? No one has 'affairs,' when I am close. But I'll humor you. A month, a year, two, or a million-trillion, it makes no difference to me. You'll still fall.

–You mean fail, my lord?

–No need to repeat myself, let's play.

I held my hands out, covering the pawns in my palms. I knew Death Incarnate could see through my hands. He picked my right hand, but just pointed at it. A well-meaning, <u>sincere</u> touch from him, I'd be dead.

–You're black, I see, my lord.

–Appropriate enough but that won't save you.

–And maybe I'll play a game you've never seen before, my dark lord.

I set the game up rapidly. I sensed He wanted to get down to business.

We set up the game at an inn in Rouen. They serve wine and some kind of beer. I hated beer, and I knew the wine could do me some slight level of brain damage. I took the wine but did not drink. I set it aside. Then, I ordered coffee (or the equivalent, a stimulant).

That amused Death Incarnate.

—Coffee? In times such as these, your killing me, human and could you make it a long-kill? I'd so like that.

—Coffee is a vitamin, not a drug. Drug-free, my lord. The saurian strictures are a lot to live up to, my dark angel.

—Ah, screw that shit, bar tender, bar tender, ho! Give me a beer and keep 'em coming! When its tax time, alcohol lists me as a dependent. Funny huh, Brian? I've tried to be like you, with jokes and all. Strange my jokes fall flat, as will you, flat on your back like a pancake when I'm through! I'll be there to spread that bloody syrup on top, too.

We sat in the back, up against a lightly-stained-glass-window. Of-too-course, the three people previously sitting there in our spot now felt 'inclined' to move. Windows were rare, very rare. Death Incarnate liked that very much. He could stare out at the other people He'd be collecting anon. How could I win against the Hour Keeper when He didn't see me winning at all?

Death Incarnate had his dark, slouch hat on with a very, very wide brim, the sad sorrows of quarantine, mankind's illnesses, and human suffering written all over Him, pandemic just forever (more). I'd rather visit Hell than sit with this dangerous angel over a game of chess. Death Incarnate looked at me, then languidly moved his pieces around to the center of each square, in set-up mode.

—I'll collect them all. Those people out there, I mean. Look how oblivious they are, they actually think that this universe is just for them, they don't think of me at all, in their short, extremely brief, time. Yet me or my minions will collect. No escape, and the nothingness that awaits them all, <u>that</u> is epic, yes?

I disregarded what I didn't understand (or was afraid to comprehend).

–Maybe not 'nothing,' my lord if—

–Your beliefs, like your world, is a secret abyss.

–Stroke notwithstanding, I read John L. Watson's <u>Secrets of Modern Chess Strategy</u> last, so just watch yourself, my dark lord. I do have some recallogical problems.

Death Incarnate then scoffed, and actually laughed.

–You are being pretentious. Did you know that Paul Keres beat John Watson in Vancouver in 1975?

I didn't know any of this but played along.

–Okay, my dark lord, and I adjust my pieces, so please you.

I copied Death Incarnate manipulating my chessmen (and chess-women!) around, just a little.

–Did you know that Keres won the Vancouver tournament in that year?

–Alright.

–Keres then packed up and was headed home to Estonia, right?

–Uh-huh.

–Uh-huh, what, young man?

–Uh-huh, yes, my dark angelic lord, so please you.

–He died on the way home. I know. I was there.

A huge shutter befell the inn. The sun was dimmed. All the peasants, priests, and soldiers thought a sudden storm was looming. I knew better. I responded weakly.

–Yes, my dark lord.

The board was set up. Death Incarnate started turning his two knights around, making them harder to see (not really <u>that hard</u>, but He learned that somewhere, probably from another ((dying)) victim).

–Shall I dine on your flesh in front of your surprised face? Just sayin'.

–So please you, my lord, but let's finish the game, then, do as you please.

I didn't inform Him of my 'cure' by Littorian. He still thought his 'gracious stroke' from the Water World held me in a 'severely disabled' condition. Since I would one day become a dragon myself, I was pre-graced with Littorian's way of playing chess and my own experience.

Take Death Incarnate's knights, leaving Him with a bishop pair. Then, make inferior moves to confuse my nemesis, making Him think me weak on chess yet again. Let my Drunken Magnus opening confuse Death Incarnate. I was going to use my Polish opening (or Gorilla opening). I didn't do my Polish opening. I wish Death Incarnate to place me as a novice in His Universal-mind. Hopefully, He'll be fooled. And I definitely don't like the way He'll *and* Hell *are so close together when spelled out!*

I thought of something little known, something a little bit subtle (and maybe something more <u>*subtil*</u>)!

–Is this a <u>losing</u> chess game, my lord?

Death thought nothing about it at all.

–You'll lose and that's a sure thing.

–Sure. I understand, my lord—it's just like what you say it will be, 'losing chess,' yes. I mean, there are only 88 keys on the piano, but do you run out of music? Of course not. And there are 64 squares on a chess board, but how popular (or popularist?) is that game, yet, still? And the Chinese game 'Go' has—

–Yes, yes, I get your point, but this is chess, every move counts, because your <u>very life</u> is at stake! You will not win, and I have foreseen that, and I am <u>never wrong</u>, not for forever and a day! Let's play...to your gracious death!

Chapter Six

Dragons of Romania

Littorian and the other saurians found out about the dragons of Romania before any human. Even when we got there, Littorian scented the dragons *very being* through his human <u>nose</u>, and he knew the dragons were in trouble. That much of 'being a saurian' came through, though not much else did. At the same time, Joan's trial was proceeding to a rather dismal fate: Sure Death (and that by fire). That would be on May 30, 1431.

For my chess game with Death Incarnate, we were nearly at the end of the opening. Then I had my 'affairs' to contend with and bid adieu to my storked doctor. Death Incarnate didn't stop me, and it was my move. I was lucky he let me depart.

Our dragon-stars could sense the <u>very blood</u> of the dragons of Romania! This altered things. We had two parties to save, things grew more complicated. Joan and now the dragons, too! Even though a copious amount of blood was flowing in all the companions, they didn't 'feel' those desperate, hunted dragons in Romania, just over 1,000 miles away.

—You can sense that, right, Littorian? And they are in danger, right?

—I can, young human. They might be the last dragons on

Earth, in my diminished state I can't read any other dragons. We won't have any animal shouting matches, believe me there!

Tiperia took control of the dragon-rescue. She nodded to Littorian and they made rapid, beyond speed-of-light, plans. She flew all of us to Romania on her mighty dragon back. And indeed, she'd shuttle us back and forth, so all shape-shifters had time to meet with the dragons. She didn't mind creating a magical atmosphere around everyone and anyone giving us some 'dragon-face-time.' Tiperia explained saurian companionship with the human teenagers, and the dragons were completely fascinated. Not violent but interested all the same. They nodded when the 'scent' of dragons was learned by the shape-shifters. Only Tiperia could act as a dragon and not have to 'shortly' go back through time. Rules didn't apply to this particular 'god.' No wonder she was in charge of the dual-rescue, Joan of Arc and the endangered dragons.

In the time it's taken to read this, the dragons were negotiating with Tiperia and the danger before them was outlined.

Villagers.

Villagers wished the dragons dead.

This would change our plans completely. The dragons had to be saved. If I thought things were complicated before, playing chess with Death Incarnate, well, shit was just getting started.

Chapter Seven

Shepherd Girl's Trial

Meanwhile, Bishop Cauchon applied maximum pressure to Joan for just a few reasons. Obviously, I had no sympathy for his rationales. He wanted a Cardinal's gangster-cap or a much wider bishop-**shit**-ship. The English were insistent on having the Maid burned at the stake, and appeasing 'the invaders' was Cauchon's number one priority. Too, taking on the dress of a man was enough to have her killed in a hideous way. Joan of Arc was clever with her witchcraft responses, but that cleverness wouldn't save her.

The shape-shifters took up their usual places (those not seeing the dragons in Romania), and I fit in, too. I was just a superfluous, sedulous writer, a page, with nowhere to go. We were all concerned about Joan, but what could we do, just fitting in with history? Anakimian's fiery wings, that was the answer to everyone's question *why*.

The court of inquisition was meeting. How could a 19-year-old peasant girl almost turn the tide with England, this girl threatened to bring the 100 years' war to an end, with just herself!? Armed force combined with diplomacy were the watchword of today. The Armagnacs knew this well. Obviously, the British crown wanted to make France a vassal of England (to use the medieval phrasing). Quite obviously again, Perrier Cauchon knew what his handlers desired. What could a just-post-Dark-Ages-English-favoring-Catholic-priest need anyway? I was seeing all (or almost all) so I was inching towards forgiving all. That's what Littorian thought was necessary. He was recovering nicely and didn't want to step on the same rake again regarding offending any knights. Littorian doesn't need to be taught his faults once made known.

Speaking of chess, my chess game, stopped after our opening moves now followed hard-upon. I thought, apprehensively, about Death Incarnate, too much really. Then, I saw Brother Guillaume Duval, of the Order of Saint Dominic and the Covent of Saint Jacques at Rouen. He was with Brother Ysambard de la Pierre and Maître Jean Delafontaine. They were deputized to visit Joan of Arc, too, in prison. This was in the castle of Rouen. The Earl of Warwick attacked Brother Ysambard because he was sympathizing with Joan. I watched this closely. He threatened to throw Brother Ysambard into the Seine River if he didn't cow-toe to the "English-way."

Whether some of these people were shape-shifted or not I really cannot say. If they were, then they are as history paints them.

Sheeta came to me and I listened intently.

–I'd like to talk to Joan of Arc. Jing, too.

–Getting into that prison will be difficult; I think you'd better approach it with royalty, with, maybe a Burgundian princess or someone wearing a priest's robe. Just my thoughts.

–You had a thought? That can be janky and painful for you. You think that we don't care about human life, that we all look the same, black hair, black eyes, and your view of anime have colored your outlook on all my people, Asians like violence isn't that right Brian? Ever heard of Taoism, in China? Or in our country, of

Shinto, or belief in sacred power, that is, kami? After World War Two, Shinto ended, but I'm losing my point. I'm DNA-borne, I can't change my outward appearance. Inwardly, that's what really counts!

This made me uncomfortable, this line of thinking, in myself. I tried to cover it up. I didn't want to be accused of racism. I attempted to hide it, my prejudice against Asians, but I leaked it all out when I communicated their roles to rescue Joan. I just felt like our DNA determines all (unless we are concentrating hard on it, even our thesis, antithesis and synthesis)—all that we have <u>learned</u>, not <u>know</u> through generalized experience and we have to humbly "rise above" our prejudice, as contradictory as that sounds, especially in the (non) realm of anarchism, you can't be 'two-faced' on prejudice or suffer the consequences of being someone functioning on prejudice. Even including myself, people are kinda screwed up. I'm getting better, but Sheeta wasn't helping.

–You know I'm trying to <u>learn</u> different than I <u>feel</u>. What you're saying is that I'm like Colonel Kurtz, from <u>Apocalypse Now</u>. That was based on Joseph Conrad's <u>Heart of Darkness</u>. In the movie, Kurtz said that Asians were a harder kind of people than folks in the West, because the enemy hacked-off the arms of children inoculated for polio. I think he was right about the North Vietnamese and maybe Asians in general. I realized that the Asian countries hate each other for, like, invasions that happened in the past, or, like the Nanking Massacre between the Chinese and Japanese folks in the 1930s. See that's DNA again. Maybe humanity can never 'forgive' given our DNA. The crux of that whole movie was this quote: "Drop the Bomb exterminate them all," written in marginalia on this manuscript, almost at the end, about three hours and 10 minutes in. That's why with an insane concept like war you have to kill your enemy completely—women, children, and men, then you know you've won. It's just a thesis, and I know you offer an antithesis. Maybe together we can come to a new, really new, synthesis. There is always learning in a freedom of speech collective, like our companionship deal.

Sheeta smiled.

–That learning is harder than knowing, Master Brian. You make me confront my own prejudice, only thing, it's justified, and maybe that's the Asian Achilles Heel. I'm prejudice but with good reasons. I just knew I'd like Americans for something, but why this? Remember Master Miller, history wasn't won by a tossed salad, giving a reason, doesn't clarify things. That's not the "human judgmental way." We like things to be a bit more difficult, then it's not boring.

–Alright Sheeta, well, sorry for the Boxer Rebellion, or whatever. Oh, don't mention 'America' to our country-general-girl, it'd just confuse her. She's going to have a tough time with history as it is. Let's not change her or history. And that includes her DNA!

Sheeta waved. She was off to see shape-shifted Larascena or Clareina, and they would guide her to Joan of Arc. My wives introduced Sheeta and Jing to Brother Ysambard and, at this time, he was shape-shifted into Anakimian.

Joan languished in her prison, and Jing and Sheeta tried desperately to see her. (Also, I never heard word one from Rachel or Jason, they just melded into the French scene).

The shape-shifting theologians tried to see Joan, too, but as soon has questions about <u>why</u> they wanted to see Joan, and they foreigners, they just demurred. Within less than a month before her death, they were finally given audience with the overly-exhausted Joan.

Three guards were placed against the walls. It was Brother

Ysambard that attended with the two teenagers to see Joan. Sheeta spoke first.

–It's very nice of you to see us, Jeannette.

–It wasn't my decision, people come and go, and I think mostly to mock my capture, God forgive them.

–That's not why we are here.

Joan, very much taxed, grew irritable.

–Then why, savior forbid?

Jing spoke now, getting ahead of Brother Ysambard. He wanted to talk to Joan of Arc and since he was a saurian, he wanted this in the worst way. He wanted to talk about strategy, *saving strategy*. Sheeta, for her part, sat in silence, really listening.

–We have to talk about your capture at Compiegne, my lady. You displayed an art form that we thought was reserved for our Asian people alone, but you executed it perfectly!

–Fortunately, thank God, I didn't 'execute' anyone keeping up with my record of never killing anybody. I respect Asia and I'm free of any kind of prejudice. I did knock those Burgundians around, and they definitely deserve it, by our Mother Church!

Brother Ysambard could wait no longer.

–Forgive me my question, fair maid. First, I hope they are treating you like a general?

–They are treating me like the pail I have for a wash-room, so please you; I wish the church could give me better?

–We are sourly resisted. First though: You wish to be free of this prison, right?

–I've escaped before, and can do so again, by Christ! They will soon descend me as a strumpet, that's in their hearts, any fool can see. I don't know the way to escape!

–That way will be revealed to you shortly, Joan, can you stand it, and no matter what form it takes?

At this statement, Brother Ysambard gripped his hands. He

wished to talk about a 'dragon-rescue' but didn't dare, he didn't want to frighten Joan too much. Plus, he was being listened-to. The Brother couldn't describe the coming of Anakimian, a dragon-star, and carrying her off. At least, not yet.

–I can, that you must know, my priest. I know that the English and the Burgundians want my death by way of the misguided church to be through fire, the worst death I could imagine. To think I tried to rid us of the English, that done in the name of God, you must see the good in this?

–Someone we can't see can see the 'good' in this, but, in time, you might have another perspective. All will be revealed to you, at the end. Prepare!

Jing chimed in now.

–My turn, sir Brother.

The conversation when on for a long time. Many matters were discussed, and Brother Ysambard thought Joan knew her deliverance was a hand. Could she be rescued at all? Anakimian would see it so. I'd soon know, but it wasn't how I thought it should be.

Chapter Eight

"I was the Angel"

It was late in May 1431, and the whole companionship was brisling. We were divided up now. I stayed in Rouen to see Joan at the execution of her sentence. Anakimian was on his way to get the dead girl in a farm he heard about in a distant town, and Tiperia was there to tell him when to exactly arrive at the stake. Tiperia looked like a noble Burgundian and was dressed in a white full-length gown. The dead girl was a key in our overall plan.

We stayed right with Bishop Pierre Cauchon. Tiperia detested him, couldn't stand the very Earth on which is sordid feet rested.[5] Joan had been captured near Cauchon's diocese, not in it.

---

5   Let me say this, on 'dealing' with Tiperia. First, she is Good, and that is above Truth. Let me explain, and that real briefly. Post-truth is just anti-truth, don't let anyone fool you there, so 'post' that! And this isn't an exercise in any kinda semantics, hear? Truth is relative. Good, though, isn't. The 'truth' was, 500-600-700 years ago, the Earth was flat. That was the truth, then. But now we know that's kinda false. Now we know 'better'. But what will be 'better, still' 500-600 years from now? Well, who knows? 'Good' doesn't know any 'time' or any 'distance,' Truth definitely knows something about 'time.' The Catholics said Joan was a witch in 1431 (true) and made her a Saint in 1920 (true). They can't both be 'right'. Truth is

Tiperia, knew a good deal about the humans involved, and

---

sorta "wobbly," but Good is not (at least, as I <u>currently</u> understand it; maybe, in <u>time</u> it might be different, but I don't think so!). For instance, we 'celebrate' democracy. Democracy, truth, good, right? But like Churchill said, the best argument against democracy is a five-minute talk with the average voter. That's just devastating— and maybe that's the truth. You just shouldn't even trust people with anything especially <u>truth</u>! That's post-truth, there: The facts are shitty, so ignore them. Truth hurts and should be rejected by higher humanity, for humanitarian reasons. So, it's not at all a tautology. So Tiperia goes with anarchy. The thing is, everyone says that I want people to be dragons, too, that I want them to live forever. Now, just as a for-instance, the Crocodilians live a long time, but eventually die. But if they are really 'brothers' with the Lizardanians and the Alligatorians and drank their blood and all (the former two living forever), causing them (the Crocodilians) to live forever, too, well, the Universe is big enough for everyone, even humans living forever, and maybe as dragons. There are worse fates, not all eyes would weep for humanity. So, everyone should be a dragon-star. This is what Soreidian accuses me of. He thinks I'm arrogant and ignorant. Right on the latter, wrong on the former. I'm a teenager, that's my 'original' sin: I have a hope for life itself! I'm guilty of what Soreidian is talking about. The first stage was getting peace between all saurians. That was accomplished. Now, for Part Two. Don't worry about me, I'm most comfortable in a fight, and this is my armor, and we'll find the (dialectical) truth, together, right, reader? That is, thesis, antithesis and synthesis. It's just like saying, "I didn't mean what I meant then!" or "I was in my right mind at this synthesis". Ergo, you can see why, with time, people are crazy if, in <u>that</u> synthesis, they 'decided' witches should burn, like Joan of Arc! You evolve into a higher 'knowing.' Truth is relative, knowing just that lil' Trinity; just think of it as "SAT" backwards! And of corruption, we have "institutional corruption" which means everyone is corrupt, like Clint Eastwood said, guns she found them wanting regarding courage. She did interview Joan, and knew the girl was ignorant but she was Good. If you got a 'good' from Tiperia, she would help you. Maybe Tiperia's help was all Joan needed.

If you're just a young girl, even with divine intervention, eventually you will abandon heaven, in the face of worldly hurts. Didn't Jesus himself, on the cross, say, "My God, my God, why hast thou forsaken me?" when the pain was too great for a mere human to bear? I was there when the worn-out general said the following:

—It was I who brought the message of the crown to my King. I was the angel and there was no other.

The truth was, Joan of Arc was the first-cousin to an angel, she was a saint, and none can deny this!

Meantime, my chess game was about to conclude with Death Incarnate.

I did not win.

---

are okay as long as the right people get killed. I think this is saying humanity is inhumane overall. That's the kind of ignorance that is all human-borne. What is 'right' one day, will be 'wrong' the next, just give it (mean, cruel) time. In Clint's defense, he was saying that as Harry Callahan; actors often become what they detest (in part).

Chapter Nine

End-game, Mine

At the inn, just before Joan's death, playing our 'end game,' Death Incarnate was happy. The dark angel was so enthusiastic about the end-game with me he didn't notice *what* I was doing. I was playing him my "Drunken Magnus" approach. If you need to know what that is, just Google it (+"chess"). So there.

The "Doctor" and I had this end-game at the inn, in a very-much forgotten corner. He was beside himself, and, I admit, the "doctor" was not attune to the saurian spell I had on him. He had beer by the pints, but nothing could affect him that way, of course. Death Incarnate didn't know I had a saurian-mind-melt working on him, in a very subtle way! This was very dangerous, and believe me, I had to! He was greedy, and I keyed on that, making him just get greedier, forcing his pawns to become queens.[6] Even with

---

[6]   Here's the thing about chess, one of my 'trainings' with saurians. I was of the opinion that there was only one woman, the Queen, for each side, on any given chess board. The Saurians told me I was really wrong. I had nine women on my side of the board, eight women-bees, and one Queen Bee. When they get to the other side of the board, what do you think they are, a cross-dresser like Joan of Arc? Nah. They are women all the while! Who knew? Saurians

all his eons of existence, he didn't see the snare, getting his pawns Queened.

–Queen me, fool human! Taste death, you'll hollow and wallow in it, oh, the dark blood, the veins, my horror! Oh, you will know it all!

I tried not to imagine his cruel forms of death for me. I put Death Incarnates' queen back on the board in silence, but I was shaken and visibly shivered. Beneath the stork, hideous changes must have been taking place, victory was so great, such an abyss of absolute death, that is, *my death*. I innocently moved a pawn up, it was blocked by his sole bishop, though. Death Incarnate was nearly in hysterics. He moved up another pawn for her queen-ship.

–Queen it, queen it, and get ready to die!

No one in the bar was watching the bird-peaked-doctor, they had us on total-ignore. I set a rook up-side-down, which was a traditional way for another queen. Death Incarnate was really fascinated by the 'rook-on-rear,' and wanted the same thing yet again! Raging like he was orgasming right on the chess board, Death Incarnate was blinded by over-victory.

For my turn, at games' end, I had three pawns left. Death Incarnate had no need to conceive what I was doing, I had all my pieces up against his black pieces, only my king could move. Still, he moved up another pawn to its end-goal.

–Queen it, queen it, damn-you-queen-it, and now, little human I'm going to get you to—

Instantly I placed my soul remaining black rook upside down and interrupted Him and this was my sole, bold move.

–You got me, my lord, but oh, isn't that a stalemate? My king can't move at all now, if you'll take notice. You see, my pawn is

---

do, I guess. The women outnumber the men! Just like today? Well, maybe not so much.

up against your bishop now, all my other pawns similarly blocked, too, it's my move, and I don't have anywhere to move! I'm not in check. Boy, you just got too many queens on the board, my lord, wow, three black queens. I can't make a move, lest I'd be in check. Some people wouldn't call this a draw, they'd ignorantly give me the game. Can you believe people would do that? You said we were playing Loss Chess, Suicide Chess or Losums, which is like Take-All chess, and stalemate is a win for the stalemated player. I think we were just playing regular chess, but who am I to know? If I hadn't represented, well damn, taking our pieces off the board when we just wanted to, it couldn't be that—

Now, I stopped talking because his bone-thin hand hammered down on the table, making the very floor jump under my feet, really the whole building rocked! Flabbergasted, Death Incarnate looked at the completeness of the board for the first time. His folly was clear to see. Death Incarnate was so <u>fixed</u> on roasting me alive, he didn't see the <u>entirety</u> of the chess board, and my narrowing position within it! He looked at me with evil only Death would know. Luckily his face was like a bird's, otherwise, it would be unbelievably insane and obscene.

–Get out. You're free.

–My dark lord if you think—

–I said get out! You stinking, unknown back-bencher, go! Time will pass, something will happen. Get! Get! Or I'll sting your miserable feet!

Obviously, you should do what Death tells you to do, J.R.R. Tolkien be damned!

I got up.

Looking again at the chess board, my brave white king, I swear, was melting, literally, in front of my frightened eyes. He'd performed so nobly, but he was sacrificed at the end, but not really! He didn't end up in checkmate, I saw to this. Death Incarnate was threatening a typhoon of rage, gazing at the chess board with so much incredulity. I thought everything on the whole board would totally disinter, go to pieces in this reality, at his Death-stare.

I left the room, heading back to Rouen.

As the sun smacked its lowered bloody lip to the horizon, I knew I dodged a fatal bullet. That bullet was more like a boomerang, I found out. I managed to find my wives, Lara and Clare, and slept by them.

I whispered to them.

—Beauty fades, but dumbness is forever. I guess that extends to Death Incarnate.

I thought they could protect me with their dragon-minds. Thing is, they were shape-shifted, and were quite asleep. I had horrible nightmares, and that seemed to last forever.

Just before I left Rouen, when the sun was almost down, as I left town to go to the castle, I got five-flagged in my unsuspecting face. It'd been a long time since someone punched me. But it was a human's sock, it didn't 'knock my block off,' like a saurian's talon-filled strike would do.

Oh, no.

I didn't even fall or stagger back. It was full in the face, but no blood issued forth from my lips. I had the blood of three leading dragons in me now, and that wasn't affected by my travel-in-time, and <u>someone</u> was going to get-it-<u>bigly</u>!

—Now we can have that fight, Brian. I'm going to make you suffer, but good. I just wish Danillia was here, she'd like this very much.

It was the shape-shifted Soreidian. He'd changed into a priest, no less! He was bald as a harsh purge, too.

—Just my chance to lash out at the Catholic Church, thank you Soreidian, you cheeky shill!

The faux-priest smiled.

–Correlation doesn't equal causation, Brian.

–In this case, it does, and I'm going to kick your Catholic correlation butt!

–And you, un-cultured sodomite, come on!

–You shape-shifted piece of shit, stepping on my every-punch-line, you'd betta recognized my gangsta, Soreidian!

The shape-shifter thought he was <u>still</u> a dragon-star, almost invincible. As Soreidian he certainly was. Now, not so much at all. I sent all my Black weapons away, with a wink to them. And so did Soreidian! The worst move he's ever made. He had no mental ability to call his Black Sword and other weapons back! His Black Sword knew this, but the shape-shifted dragon didn't.

Weapons dismissed (my own Black World sword with a snicker and wink), the priest hit me three times in the stomach, three in the face, full force. My abs were very strong, and still no blood peppered my face.

–That'd be it? This is for Joan of Arc!

I hit the shape-shifted priest and he landed 10 feet away. I wasn't done with him yet.

Half unconscious at my first blow, I straddled his chest and hit him continuously in the face. I could have punched him through the ground completely, making a grave for him right there, but I held back. Splattering his mug, I made stirred-up strawberry pie out of his vulnerable jaw.

When his cheek bone did appear, caked in milky-blood, I stopped. My dragon veins said to finish him, my humanity held me at bay. If he died here in the past, he'd never live as a dragon again. I knew that, but 'absolute violence' was not in me; some violence, that, but not enough to finish anyone.

I got up.

Soreidian didn't.

He was barely conscious. He tried to rise but couldn't, his black robes red, too.

–Come on don't get up for me. I've got the most powerful saurian blood in my bones—and Littorian's too. An ode to Lara. I hope you've learned something about being hurt like all-buggery, Soreidian. You're a little French human here-and-now, so get used to it. Shape-shifted, you've got no dragon in you at all! I'll send you back some help, damn, you need it. *You just got pwned*!

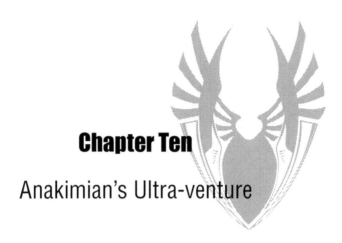

Chapter Ten

Anakimian's Ultra-venture

Death Incarnate was standing alone, in a field outside of Rouen, and it was the 30th of May 1431. He accepted a stalemate, which wasn't what he considered a draw. Really, I won the game and 'declared' a stalemate because of his 'bad' moves!

As a consolation, he thought he'd be seeing Joan of Arc, before too long. Boy, if he knew the true intentions of the saurians, not to just <u>see</u> this Saint, but to <u>save</u> her!

Death was upset by our chess game. This was a 'draw' and <u>that</u> from a human? He must be playing like a computer, that's all he could figure from my play. Death—the Dark Angel—had a double-beef with me. In his way, Death Incarnate would have his revenge, and that anon!

The Hour Keeper, forlorn over his 'draw' to me in that chess game, raised a hand at the flying reptilian. This is what He must have been thinking.

That god-damned child, that Brian Miller, I should have known they'd bless him (or curse him?) with saurian abilities as well as healing him. How could I have been so stupid? Oh, that's it. He had a spell on me, a saurian spell? I thought that stroke would be decimating, would cut his mind in half! Now, I see Brian covered up his renewed-brain with Lizardanian thoughts just to deceive me. He reflected his past-mind on me, and I bought it. Yes, saurians are subtle and subtil as said in Genesis. And you'd think Death Incarnate would know such. Brian Miller is essentially a dragon, but I'm not done yet!

That's what Death Incarnate must have been thinking. Or something like that. The Hour Keeper and I never exchanged actual thoughts—

Death Incarnate let his hand down.

–Now, my little dragon, you have some <u>fun</u> with that!

Anakimian, with his very light burden, was feeling energized, assured that he'd have Joan of Arc riding him before long. Anakimian was overjoyed; it'd all be over soon. He tolerated things as a shape-shifter, but really, he didn't like it too much; he felt awkward the entire time. It'd be worth it, getting Joan as a companion, and, maybe, making her the "Lead Companion." First, the rescue, and the rest would follow.

Anakimian wasn't violating any 'rules' of time-travel turning into a dragon-star now. He'd soon be out of there, and all the historical stuff would be the same anyway. He was aware of the Dragons of Romania and figured Tiperia would make it all 'come together' like a referee calling a big game. Anakimian was concerned with Joan and his imagination took him no further than saving that peasant angel. Too, my position with Death Incarnate didn't bother him in the least, indeed he wasn't aware of it. Really, no one was. I didn't burden anyone with Death Incarnate, but he made his presence known anyway.

The young teenager in his claws died from the plague. The little family put the body out in the barn. No one saw the saurian go in. No one saw him leave. As he flew along, Anakimian had to physically check his clawed hands to see if he even <u>had</u> a girl, she was so spindly and light.

Speeding at next-to-warp-flight, Anakimian had plenty of time to save Joan, or so he thought to me, later on. The reptilian actually thought he'd come off well, just chuckling to himself, carrying his feather-weight burden in his mammoth claws. He actually slowed down now, guided by Tiperia's telepathy. Anakimian gave me his thoughts, thereafter.

I should get my little plague-hen to the site, but not too quick! Thank goodness Tiperia is there, she'll have me show up just in time. The fire must be all around our little teen idol, then I'll just swoop down and then use the wind afterward, to cool Joan. I will tie my poor little deceased peasant to the stake on the platform, all it a whirl, then take my pious little angel off, then away. All of this, at light speed! I know just where to 'sit' my companion, oh, yes, on my sinuous back. Things couldn't be more perfect! Sometimes I amaze even my muscled-self and then some!

Anakimian was almost giggling, communicating closely with Tiperia as to the exact second to arrive at Joan of Arc's pyre. The saurian felt a twitch in the girl he held in his mammoth clawed hands. She was vigorously pawing the young Alligatorian now, scratching him, squirming around, 400 feet up, with only a few minutes to go before Joan's rescue. Naturally, Anakimian could squish her up like an accordion, but he thought 'enforced learning' at this late hour would suffice. He knew about dealing with a medieval girl, anyway, from Joan. Anakimian was completely alarmed, I have to say, and, with his eagle eyes, he saw the sinister, satisfied look of Death Incarnate just before He faded away.

A-ha, that's it. Death Incarnate lashing out at Brian Miller, obviously, and I'm the victim! So much for just <u>watching</u> Joan of Arc getting burned, which is what Death Incarnate thought we'd be *doing. Well, I can see where He'd be pissed. Damn, Brian's a little snake-and-a-half!*

The great reptilian was very put-out and didn't even think to give the girl a verbal reassurance. Especially with her randomly scratching him at every turn. The Alligatorian <u>forced</u> telepathy on the girl's mind, with background and foreground all thrown in for good measure. She knew his complete story and how he tried to help Joan through her plight. Here was a rare use of the superiority of the saurian mind, bringing an understanding to this resurrected child. Anakimian could bring a knowing, an *understanding*, to the post-Dark Ages lass, and it was 'just so' in the time it's taken you to read this. And that's not Post-Truth, either!

Then, the girl in Anakimian's mighty claws was silent. Her arms dropped, she stopped calling out to the heavens, angels, everything unearthly. A sudden comprehension smote the teenager and she didn't interrupt the creature carrying her.

–So, <u>all</u> of this is clear to you now, like a summer rain, on a typically French day?

–Yes, and really, it's true, to know all is to forgive all. I'd really like to meet Littorian, the Lord of the Lizardanians sometime, he's so wise! I see it all now, or at least some. I forgive you for this, but I'm not sure what is making me…alive right now, my, uh, my lord dragon?

–Death Incarnate has willed it, obviously to get back at Brian Miller. They must have had a bargain, and Brian Miller is known for doing that kind of stuff, and Death came off worse! This is a fine-tuned operation, and Brian's little deals with Death Incarnate are really a hindrance. Details for another time, when we can both learn of them. Right away, it's Joan of Arc that awaits us. You see the need?

Anakimian was combining patience with a need to get to Joan in only a few minutes.

—I do see what she wants, and I've heard of her too. Yes, use my life to save her. I'm just a peasant girl, of no use, I'd gladly sacrifice myself for Jeanette d'arc, of course! Maybe you thought differently of me, but that's the way I feel, Messier Dragon. By the way, you are built, my lord, I've never seen so much outrageous, gorgeous muscle.

Anakimian was quite entertained by the girl's spirited responses.

—I'm Anakimian, an Alligatorian, and it's nice to meet you. Yes, I'm strapping, you should see me on strength-display and of that, later. Sorry about my 'forced learning' on you, just now, but we definitely don't have time for any proper Meet-and-Gracious. Not that I'm asking you to bow down before my dragon-self, but if you feel the need, just wait until we are on the ground. I'm authenticating you, announcing my awesome power of the dragon-star, just *ta-da*!

He gripped her on the left side of her ribs, trying to support her completely, and reached a massive right hand around to her, in greeting.

She gripped two of his claws in her hand, all she could grab. Anakimian was thoughtful about penetrating her skin with his seven-inch claws.

—So, we will defy the Hour Turner. You're name?

—It's simple, as I am, it's Darcey, my dragon lord.

—I see. As you know, I'll be the companion to Joan of Arc, if we manage to save her. You will take Joan's place. So, you have to die. And I'm more than sorry about this.

As I heard it from Anakimian, there was no delay in Darcey's answer.

—Make my death quick, my lord. I admire Joan of Arc very

much. Joan of Arc is what the English call her, anyway. This is my especial privilege to die for her.

This made Anakimian think for a short while, as he carried Darcey along in the brisk wind. He noticed her necklace.

–Give me that necklace, child. Wrap it around my neck, if you please, I think it's barely long enough. Can you throw out the lavender inside it? Right, empty, and with a little clasp there, yes, seal that, if you please.

Awkwardly, the girl did as she was told.

–Alright, Darcey, this is important. And you are very compliant, you see Joan headed to the pyre, in my mind?

–I do my lord. Yes, I'd give my life to save Joan, just take it, if it's not too much of an ask.

–Death Incarnate failed there I guess, my child. He's done a deed, but human freedom he <u>doesn't</u> control, as God Almighty doesn't, am I right there?

–You are right, my dragon lord, but I don't want so much as a sin against God, here at the end.

–It's not going to be the end, my girl. No sin against God, that's for sure. You've some wit, human, I'll tell you that much. Here's what: I'll take your heart, your soul, your mind, all of you, and place it in this little, wooden heart-shaped box. Then, when we get to the future, I will revive you in another body. In addition, I'll have a companion for you, a star dragon, a certain young Alligatorian, Anaphielian. He's in need of a companion, just now. Anaphielian is young, you'll get along fine. He will want you, because I've examined your mind, and will share that with him. Can you live as a companion?

–Like Katrina and Brian and all of the companion humans you've shared with me mentally?

–Like them, *only better.* Doing this for Joan, you'll be overfilled with love, and from a dragon, that is saying something. You will drink the blood of an Alligatorian, and live forever, too. I promise this to you, and there is so much more, but I haven't got all day to tell you of it. In fact, Joan's got only minutes left.

–Can I make a request, my dragon?

–Anything you please.

–I wish to serve Joan. As you know, this is a saint that does not know that she is! And that's a Saint's Fate, lord dragon.

–Serve Joan? As a slave, or something?

–I wish to companion with Joan, my dragon-star, just as you companion with Joan in your own way.

–That's granted, and right away, too.

The little girl took a breath, there in the ultra-claws of Anakimian. The next town was Rouen, Darcey could see it on the horizon. Then, she shook.

–Will it hurt much?

–Once done, in the next moment, you'll be alive in a human body, and all of your memories will be with you, all you've learned and thought, that I guarantee, Darcey. All you learned here, will be with you then!

–Will I see you again, Anakimian?

–I'll be the first face you see, child, believe this.

–I'm more than ready.

At that, Anakimian broke her neck in the kindliest way possible. She felt no pain, and I don't know how that happened, maybe by magic, which was a mercy.

Chapter Eleven

Our Saint's Fiery Dissemination

When Trinity Sunday came, Anakimian was playing Maitre Jean Massieu, a priest (a good priest, by the way). He told me he'd shape-shifted into others close to Joan, giving her counsel and trying to get to know her better. He did succeed in that, and the saurian liked Joan very much. In that avenue, the mission was successful, to bring Joan and Anakimian together.

Now that I had given Death Incarnate a stalemate and survived, I was reasonably happy. I didn't know that Death Incarnate was less than reasonable about our chess game and would make Anakimian pay.

Maitre Jean Massieu did relate to me that on Trinity Sunday, the English took away from Joan her woman's garment and gave her men's clothing again. After this, Anakimian did go and get Darcey. Joan had recanted, the church militant would deal with the girl-general. On Wednesday, she was led to the market place, and despite her lamentations, she asked for a cross, which she placed in her bosom.

At Rouen, I was looking for Tiperia. All of the other shape-shifters were gone, too. And no one seemed to notice the 'absence' of shape-shifters, people were as they always were! Everyone was focused on Joan of Arc and the pyre.

The crowd, some yelling, some going a little crazy with religious shouting, all around me. Tiperia was taking her own sweet time on returning everyone, I thought hastily, to the future. I was in the middle of the crowd now. Burgundians, English, and some selection of the crowd made me shy away, their repellent nature had me near-choking. I would have made a fortune selling deodorant. Where was Tiperia? I looked for the lady-in-white, couldn't see her. All depended on her guiding Anakimian to the stake.

Joan approached with her guards. They were English and a nasty bunch, too. They shooed away the crowd, I put my hand on my Black Sword.

If Tiperia doesn't show up, I'll have to do it myself, but nothing is possible without all of you Black weapons being there, okay?

My female Black Sword spirited right up. For me, I felt like I could take on a quarter of the crowd. My right-hand-hatchet, with his soul returned, encouraged me, too:

I will be there for you, Brian, but pray it shouldn't come to that. They'd see you, of course, then what would history say?

History or Her-story, huh? I just can't see her die again, I just won't have it.

At the end, Joan of Arc was relatively stolid, and walked very slowly to her death. They wrapped the Maid with ropes, bonds that were nothing to a dragon-star, of course. To the angel-teen, it was terrifying enough.

As the flames increased around Joan, I had the strength of 20 men, or more, I could save her myself. I saw a route to get her immediately. But what if one arrow-shot should find Joan? She'd been wounded two or three times before this and was appropriately weakened. The English guards could barely get her on the scaffold! My role was as a minor page, so I stood there with a pencil and my tablet.

I saw the flames rising and the smoke almost completely covered Joan of Arc. The shape-shifted saurians didn't want me interfering with the Chosen servant. They weren't around now. I so wanted to, but I didn't. My Black Sword and those Black weapons quivered noticeably on me but didn't 'draw themselves.'

Of a quick-sudden, Terminus' and Sheeta's Black World weapons, on guard then and watching Joan, just all disappeared, apparently called! I was shocked and forced myself to do nothing. Only Terminus as a dragon-star could do this, so that meant they were leaving the past right then! They went in Time and Space with their companions, too, all the way to distant Romania (and maybe beyond that, at least, I hope so).

The Black Sword looked to the crowd and was making extreme calculations. She probably was interested in not hurting anyone. Boy, the spankings and whoopings-large she could give!

Someone touched my arm with assurance.

–Oh, thank God it's you, Tip—

But it wasn't Tiperia. All my breath went out of me. It was Death Incarnate! The Hour Keeper was withdrawing all the genius-piss out of me, right then.

–Isn't it a pleasure to see you again, Brian? Play any chess, my saurian-minded teenager? I should have known that reptilian consciousness infected you, damn that Littorian to hell! I couldn't let you go and to hell with that 'draw' in chess, we've got to go to—

Of-a-sudden, Tiperia walked through the noisy crowd, and

strongly seized my other arm, and addressed Death Incarnate, roughly getting in front of me. I felt like a companion piñata.

–Of, pleasures, mine! I've business to discuss with you, Death Incarnate. There's a break in this human chaos, just there? Let this human go for now. He's not going anywhere. Shall we?

Maybe it was Tiperia's voice, (the voice of a distant star or a forlorn hope?) Death Incarnate let me go. The two of them stepped away and had a discussion.

The two reached a conclusion and Death Incarnate faded away. I wanted to know what was 'concluded' and thought to ask her. Tiperia just put up a hand, waiving me away, covering her mouth. She looked sad. Then, she made a little Air Force salute. I didn't know why Tiperia did this…until later.

At once, Joan of Arc shouted.

–Jesus! Jesus! Jesus!

Tiperia was quick as a wink.

Now, this is the moment!

Tiperia waved her hand.

It happened rapidly.

The girl's head dropped, and the flames consumed her flesh, on the pyre, all to see. I did see a flash, and that was Anakimian getting Joan out of the fire, but I was looking for it, too. The crowd was in some kind of prolonged anguish, interestingly, about three-quarters of them looking away! A soldier did see the dragon, thought it was a dove flying up, up and away. Tiperia then slapped her hands together with a loud clap. I didn't expect that out of her.

Well, I'm going to take a nap now, kinda a long day for me! Glad that's over.

Tiperia said it all playfully in telepathy to me. With Anakimian gone with Joan (allegedly), the Starfinder was going to take a nap? I wasn't even sure the event had really happened!

This human body I can't tax too much, Brian! Sure, it's in good shape but a nap is my due, my mind is to the breaking point, telepathy-wise and that Alligatorian required constant updates. It's hard communicating with a dragon-star with needs, I know. By the way, can't wait to see Littorian again, I'm due a riotous session, also!

Joan was in Anakimian's claws. Soon, she became aware, and struggled up onto his back, holding on to his fin. Her whispers to God stopped. Anakimian thought to the mind of Joan of Arc, about companionship, and just a sprinkling and splattering of things about being a companion. Almost in divine answer to her heaven-send raptures, her body cooled down appreciably. The wind was cold, and there was no 'magically-applied atmosphere' around Joan. Anakimian thought that'd be best, to start. They were flying along at 150 miles per hour, the cooling-power of the wind well at hand.

–Alright, now, my Benign Gladiator? I don't want you looking like an ice sculpture. To think I have the teenager with so many stories and films so-holy-wow! Can I establish an atmosphere around you?

The dragon-star was a God-send, Joan later told me. She was inches away from getting second or maybe third degree burns when she was talon-seized.

–An atmosphere? Films, books? Your words, my lord, say nothing. Thank you for that thought-form, I understand some of what's going on, only enough to get me into trouble. Oh, I can't go back and say good-by to my family, Anakimian?

–Well, I don't know. I guess no one would <u>believe</u> that you did come back and wish them farewell, but wouldn't that be hard on them, losing you a second time? You see that heart-shaped box around my neck?

–I guess you're right. History will take care of me? I'll hold to that, and your noble fin, too. Yes, I see the box, very pretty, so please God.

–Inside is the soul of the girl that took your place.

–What is to happen to her, my dragon lord?

–She wishes to be your companion, in addition to me. I don't mind sharing you. We have to get her another body, though. Here, let me just *think* (using telepathy, of course) of those dual-missions! Now. That's done! You and the dragons safely home! Like Brian says, 'ain't it cool'?

Like any and every teenager, she ignored what she didn't understand.

–Dragons! A full load awaits me, right? Alors ma peie j'ai peur, maman!

Anakimian laughed, with his companion-burdened on his sinuous back. I thought a love was being created, but who am I to say? If you saw Anakimian, well, then you'd know.

–More than this, Jehanette!

Chapter Twelve

Dragons of Romania Ablaze!

Almost at the same time, Littorian in shape-shifted form, was talking to the Elder Dragon, as I understand it. The Elder Dragon, was Iyarian. His wife, Itrailian. The kids, were kinda rambunctious and excitable. One (Ford truck-size) was a male, Mesrielian. His sister, sorta like a large off-roader-size-wise, Talian, was wide-eyed at the shape-shifted 'humans.' She was very, very bright, and knew not to hurt the shape-shifters (not that the Black World Weapons would allow it). She was comfortable with Tiperia, sort of a grandmotherly figure to the youngers.

Just as quick, Tiperia explained the grim history of Joan of Arc and the dragons listened. The two dragon kids were as silent as the just-covered-up-grave. Then, she explained the villagers' point of view.

Only Itrailian spoke against that dragon history, and that with anger.

–I defy such a history, and who says it has to be like that? I say we either leave or fight the villagers with a viciousness making dragons famous-forever-more!

Littorian listened and was about to say something, even rose for the event. Iyarian cut him off, though.

–No, I think <u>all</u> the dragons should go; I'll stay.

Itrailian was flabbergasted.

–What?! That's just asinine!

Itrailian's vitriol is definitely saying something, it's not good for a teenager to watch a dragon losing it. Littorian was thunderstruck, too.

–If that's the way it is, we have no argument about what must happen, my wife. You are young, I'm old, nearly spent, it's fitting that I should die here. You, all of you, dragons, companions, shape-shifters, just go on; hell, the kids are almost old enough to set out on their own anyway.

Sheeta and Terminus were concerned. The Japanese girl and her shape-shifted companion made their presence known now. Terminus had his <u>own</u> resolve to state.

–Both Sheeta and I will try to convince Iyarian that there is another way. I've already discussed it with Littorian. We will stay with him. Everyone else, just go on, you three dragons, too. Better to lose one of you than all four dragons. Tiperia, you'll see to it?

Tiperia, in dragon form, knelt down, indicating, all aboard.

–Yes I will and he's right, my friends. Joan has relapsed, and this day is going to be executed. I have to be in Rouen to direct traffic. The Black World swords are all there, just in case, the girl so fears the fire! All of you, come with me now. You'll travel back in time, we can't wait. Brian is waiting by Joan, I must go to him, soon. Littorian, Larascena, Clareina, all of you companions and saurians, I have to get you home, first. Hopefully, you've taught Joan all she needs to know. You, too, Soreidian. As for Sheeta and Terminus there is nothing I can do for them. I think their decision is foolish, but I've no time for this.

The villagers came up the mountain, and that right on time. They'd reconnoitered the exact spot of the Dragon's dwelling, earlier on. In Rouen, this was Joan's last day on Earth, and the dragon's too!

It was 30 May 1431 and the sun was laughingly dull. There were at least 250 villagers, struggling up, some just returned from the Crusades, very hard, very cruel villagers, all. They wanted to kill dragons. The villagers were quick to judge, quick to anger; slow to comprehend and didn't (not couldn't) understand that the dragons were the last remainders from pre-historic times. Their ignorance, prejudice, and fear were walking hand-in-hand as they approached the main dragon cave.

The fight between the villagers and the Elder dragon, Sheeta and Terminus was very violent. Immediately, the defenders were crippled by two arrows finding home in the torso and the right leg of Sheeta. Previously, she's submerged point down at least 80 arrows into the ground. She alighted behind them, and despite the wounds, drawing arrow after arrow, blasted them through the heads and faces of the villagers. She battled so bravely, killing at least 50 villagers with her arrows. Sheeta fought hand-to-hand, too, and none survived her kicks and hits. The love of the endangered dragon overwhelmed Sheeta.

Spears were thrown at the Elder dragon. Sheeta blocked one spear with an arrow shot, in a complex maneuver actually spinning around and going backwards, in a head-over-heals summersault. She couldn't have done this without dragon blood, she assured me with one of her last thoughts (distance-be-damned).

Terminus fought in a similar manner, but he lacked any dragon talents that Sheeta liberally employed. In the melee, a random sword deflected from Terminus' helmet, found his left clavicle and broke the bone right through. Terminus was the trios' lone foot soldier, taking on 15 to 20 villagers at once! Unfortunately, the Black World weapons were all at Joan of Arc's trial, the need to bring them not perceived. They would have made short-work of the villagers. They were held back to defend the herald of God if everything went south. That was another of the myriad deficiencies of our plan. The two humans had conventional weapons only.

The dragon pulled-off limbs and splattered matts of blood-bogged-hair everywhere. The Elder dragon took on 20 villagers at once. He was a violent dragon, blood all over the place, but, alas, he was no saurian. He did put on a dragon-horror-show to be sure.

The dragon, with spears sticking out of his hide cried in Universalian.

–You have done enough, my friend, you should go now, I know you have the dragon-power to run, so run, Terminus!

–I can fight on! Sheeta, you with me?

–I'm here, these wounds are nothing. I've arrows for every vile villager, times two, I say go on!

That was a lie, Sheeta's arrows were running desperately low. She fought so bravely, kung-fu and karate thrown randomly about (she'd learned so much from Jing), Sheeta's knives spent in the faces of two vile villagers, her sword in someone's guts, and Iyarian knew his two human friends would rather die than leave the dragon to his fate. His respect for humans took such a leap forward, and that at the end!

Then, an arrow ran into Sheeta's left forearm. Sheeta saw the shaft quivering away like a ship in a storm, the bone clearly broken. She blocked two arrows sent at her, twanging them both on the tortured ground. She had drunk star-dragon blood too and had more fight in her. With a will-unknown, she drew another arrow. All her remaining arrows found their marks in the unfortunate villagers. However, there were just too many.

Sheeta's blood was becoming a river now. Iyarian knew that Terminus' wounds were as nothing to the shape-shifter, and that he'd bleed out, too. Terminus swung his blade, dripping with copious blood, back and forth in the storm of the dragon's would-be killers.

The dragon's breath was running out too, the hydrogen in his lungs was ebbing. He'd killed at least 30 villagers with fire, and so the dragon geared up, breathing his last fire-death on two hiding behind a boulder. The concretized boulder melted, and Sheeta killed them with her remaining arrows. With her last arrow, she smote the cranium of an archer, then threw her bow at a swordsman, tripping him up, handing him a ride in the forlorn dirt. Sheeta bit down her lip at the pain, then broke the tip of the arrow in her forearm, grapping at the one knife she had left.

–Sheeta's near death, you can't let your companion die! I'm going into the cave, heed what I say!! Thank you, Terminus, but my fate, is sealed, even a dragon so mighty as you, well, just take the girl with my dear complements and fly! A saurian's got to be some place and <u>your place</u> isn't here!

Terminus then felt a heavy wound in his stomach. An arrow stood, quivering out of him, and actually poked out of his back. He was done, falling to one knee, blood poured out of him. Sheeta hobbled over to the Crocodilian, wished to be with Terminus, at the end. Another arrow in her calf, as she limped over. That was the seventh arrow in her body, and she still had some last fight in her.

–All you've got? Come on then!

With that, Sheeta found the throat of a villager with her final knife, at a distance of 40 yards. He clutched his throat, then fell dead, catalepsy-jumbo! And still the villagers came. Terminus turned to the spear-ridden serpent.

–My dragon friend, I can't, Iyarian I'm—

–Go, go, by all the gods as only a star dragon can, fly, fly!

In profound remorse and in a flash, Sheeta and Terminus

warped out on his dragon-star talons; both gone to such a world at the edge of a Universe that no one knew. The Black World weapons arrived in a flash, too, and flew with them. The villagers were blown back by the wind.

That was the last thought I had from Sheeta, I see all the images vividly. Damn I hope they are alright.

With that, the dragon when into his cave, the villagers literally on his tail, and only <u>history</u> records the reasons why.

Chapter Thirteen

Time-Traveling Dragons

Rescue made, the dragons back on "our" Earth, Joan safe and with her companion, Death Incarnate still at bay, but I would just die to know: What was concluded between the Star Finder and the Hour Wielder?

–Forgive me, Brian, but it is better that you not know. Things, didn't go as planned. Geez, even for a god what does? That devil-Death is just trying to take advantage. Please don't worry about it. Remember, perfect paranoia is perfect preparedness.

–I'll be the judge of just that, my lady Tiperia?

Flying along with the Star Finder, through Time itself, was a real treat, I remember. Everything was starlight, and a brilliant rainbow gathered all around us then. I was glad the mission, both missions, came off so successfully. Little did I know, there was a cost.

–Call it teenager-curiosity, your agreement with Death Incarnate was…?

–You don't want to fall off of me, right? Shit, you've signed so many deals with the devil, He's got tunnel-carpal syndrome. Permit a lady her secrets, and don't bojangle to me, right, I'm not a sycophantic dragon, not me.

–Alright Tiperia, you've won the day.

–Oh, have I? Don't I always? Just call it a Pyrrhic victory, sing a song for me, sometime? Is that violating a Commandment? Adventure without fear of death, talk about boring!

The dragons, meanwhile, surviving the Romanian experience, were happy to be 'in the present,' but sad, too. They were decreased by one and they all visibly pined for that being, the father-dragon. We were crestfallen too, losing Sheeta and Terminus.

Now there were three dragons at the Everglades, and it was a very awkward situation for me. For instance, the dragon-stars were fond of eating fish and 'everything in the sea' and that was fine. However, my Black World weapons were at sixes-and-sevens because these dragons wanted bison, as many a deer as could be served, cows, maybe large horses—something big and preferably bloody, too. I lobbied for them to get off Earth and to a saurian planet immediately. Someone else could worry about feeding them.

Even certain humans looked a little bit tasty, when they first arrived. I had to get all the humans off the 'base' just temporarily. Seeing the dragons and them licking their massive teeth, the companions dutifully complied. Ensconced in the Everglades in Florida, the three dragons were immediately set-upon by the saurians, politicking with them in the extreme.

Larascena made the case for the dragons settling in Alligatoria. Soreidian spoke of Lizardania were the dragons would be cared for in the extreme. Lastly, Turinian, Lord of the Crocodilians, said they'd be much better off in Crocodilia, where FIRE existed, and that would put them very much at home.

The dragons looked at the three expectant saurian presenters and winked. Three dragons, three planets. Case settled.

The dragons made it back with the companionship, to Earth. The first one they saw when materializing was complete was

Kerok! He was the only creature who didn't look surprised at seeing them. Companion Nausicaä Lee was overjoyed, too.

Kerok did notice the absence of Sheeta and her companion. I looked to him with a pained question. He smiled and gripped my shoulder with some assurance.

–They'll be alright. He's a dragon-star, after all. Forget any hope you have for now; have some dragon-faith instead!

Chapter Fourteen

Getting (Roughly) Settled

I know that Joan of Arc, after materializing at the Everglades camp, had massive 'super' problems in Florida. We were about to give up the base to the humans. All of us nearly died by Death Incarnates' sweeping hand, and I didn't like the idea of 'reflecting' on this particular adventure. I'd screwed it all up, bigly!

Joan arrived a bit cranky, seeing as how we 'drove' her (right-through) 600 years of history-plus. Her craziness is justified, seeing as how all humanity, in her brief time on Earth, let her down. Now, the saurians and the human companions considered her a Saint, causing her jaw to hit the floor with a notable clang. Joan could still smell the fire from the Catholic church on her person! Then she saw the material on her person, films, books, lectures, everything. A Saint and all this material on her? It just blew her mind.

Almost immediately after landing in the Everglades 'club,' (as the Maid like to call it), Joan of Arc, adept at English now, began reading about the "Donner Party" in my reading room. Of an evening, I found 'the General' curled up with the sleeping Anakimian reading a whole host of books brought forward by my Black World knives about the settlers in the California mountains.

Some of these books were nestled on Anakimian's face, and he ran and wrung the pages back and forth with his mighty breath. The dragon-star was quite asleep. The slight 'burning roses' scent of the saurian's breath, which wasn't overpowering at all, didn't seem to bother Joan. Whenever you're with a saurian, a human gets, well, relaxed, you get under their royal dragon-star spell. It was a very comic scene as I walked into it, with the pages blowing around by the sleeping reptilian. I saw the book under Anakimian's sleeping breath, George R. Stewart's <u>Ordeal by Hunger</u>. Anakimian must have been completely relaxed around Joan. Maybe the Donner Party had all its hopes (and faith, too) on Joan of Arc!

The companion and her dragon-star must have delved deep in my forgotten books to get so much material. I wondered why she wanted things on the Donner Party at all? Anyhow, Joan of Arc really got along well with the Alligatorian. And she owed him her life. She cooed him to sleep and in the meantime I'm not sure what 'went' on with them.

Better to leave them in privacy, but the ironwood timbers, the very firm floor boomed, boomed and boomed really continuously with 'something' going on. I didn't disturb them for a few hours of their 'booming.' I was on the ground floor of the building with my secondary office in it, and I thought the floor would cave in, damn!

Has far as Joan's reading collection, I lent the two of my Black knives to her in lieu of going to the Black World to retain her own. That, indeed, would follow hard-upon, both Anakimian and Joan needed to visit the Black World. Hopefully they'll take me and my Black World weapons along!

Oh, and forget it, if you are 'looking' for things in my testimony here, like what did Joan tell the 'discovered' dauphin convincing him to lend Joan his army and all this kinda stuff. I'm not going to give that away. Ask Joan yourself! La Hire said Joan placed artillery in a special way, though, maybe as counseled by the Archangel Michael. After she became a companion, you'd think I could question her. I really couldn't. Her privacies I respected. You would too, she really is an angel, but a veracious, avenging angel. She'll fit right in.

Chapter Fifteen

A Star Dragon's Afterword by Anakimian

Since this is my chapter, and I won't stand any interruptions like Kerok did in <u>The Theory of Saurian Anarchy</u> (I'd have scattered-on-the-wall Brian's fool-face for his puckering comments, that's for sure).

Now, then, believe me, I will be brief.

Yes, Brian, this is the young Anakimian's chapter and it'd better be <u>*right*</u>, lest I splatter your foolish-block-dizzy-head-off, right? And that "booming" business is <u>our</u> business, so let's get on![7]

Interestingly, Joan of Arc, studying exhaustively American history with her 'injections' of a certain Alligatorian's blood, proposed something to the 'time travelers.' If you think she was crazy before, you should see her after a wine glass of a saurian's plasma! The reptilians were exhausted and purposely didn't show it, as was their wont. They listened politely. The Maid wishes to go back in time to 1846 and save 'someone' from the snows of winter!

---

[7]   Oh, I don't like footnotes, either. If you have something to say, then say it, not leave it in little notes down below. Now, leave that in, too, Brian, or CRUNCH, CRACK and SQUASH!

Joan of Arc was messing around in Brian Miller's extensive library-study and was fascinated with the Oregon Trail. The general was really interested in the adventure, and how! I found books about the Donner Party everywhere, Joan of Arc littered the floor with them. My companion wished me to read all that interested her, and I dutifully did. I knew they had about 80 folks and half of them died. I read <u>The History of The Donner Party</u> by C.F. McGlashan, from 1879. There are reasonable reasons why the saurians want to leave the Earth—and how! The thing I didn't like was the journal entries. Somewhat grisly. A star dragon could right things right away, get them all out of the snowy Sierra Nevada mountains and down to California. I had to be patient with my new companion. I don't know what kind of cockamamie notion made itself known to the Maid, and I don't want to know. And I thought all of us saurians were leaving the Earth to its own fate! Of course, there is <u>always</u> Littorian, Lord of the Lizardanians. And maybe that's enough for the Earth to go its way. And the Crocodilians might have a benign solution to global warming. We'll see.

Since Joan was getting 'roughly settled' (and we did have our own adventures during these first few weeks, some of them a little tough, Joan sparring among a very surprised Florida population in a bar I won't identify[8]), I had my <u>own</u> agenda to resolve.

My small, heart-shaped box!

It was brown, very slight, and it had a Christian·cross on it, obviously hand-finished with a little knife. Since the soul of the young child, Darcey, dwelt like a child-to-be-born within, Joan, Jing, Clareina, Anaphielian and I had to go to the morgue. I felt

---

[8] But the bar is known as "Misdemeanor Meadows." I can see <u>that</u> as a footnote, not much else!

bad about Sheeta and Terminus, but I'm relying on the advice of Kerok.

Yes, the morgue! There was one of those institutions outside of Miami. The two arrived on my heavily muscled back that night at three a.m. Heavily muscled because, unlike Brian Miller, I found myself in reptilian-Herculean-excess mystifying almost all other saurians. Leave that in Brian, or CRUNCH and CRACK!!!

When we arrived at the morgue, I was put-off immediately, mind. Clareina set-down and folded her dragon wings to disappearing. This is what amazed me: You actually 'store' the dead; now that is positively Byzantine, or really Dark Ages, total yuck! Oh, of course I know about your bureaucracy, the legal proceedings that you humans have. But really! Actually, in the Dark Ages, we did see people putting the fire to bodies. Anyway, I had Jing with me, and Joan, of course. We were there to find a body for my little lassie in my heart-shaped box around my handsome, sinuous neck[9].

---

[9]   Just by the way, I have the most awesome neck of all saurians. Yes, I've even compared myself to the Wysterian Kukulkan and I do get past him, I cast longer shadows on my bulging neck muscles than even him! And you leave this footnote in, Brian, or I'll make your brain exit your mouth-almighty! Like Larascena says, 'Just so!' And If I had to 'rank' the saurians, it'd be like this (we are talking wonton-muscles-n-hugeness, hear?): Kukulkan, Teresian, Turinian, Larascena, Soreidian, Littorian, Korillia, and me. Yes, I think I could give Korillia a close run for her money (especially considering her losing that sparring match to Danillia. I heard about that, through <u>ways</u> of my own, and it <u>wasn't</u> from reading Brian's silly books that day on the Not-table, <u>The Theory of Saurian Anarchy</u>). Danillia is no slacker either, mind, she has Everett-style-muscles, I've seen those mountains on her sleek form. Korillia

Jing had me angled to a very young girl, I think she was Chinese. I'm not sure about her race and I don't really care. Jing had twittered, blogged, emailed, Googled, used telepathy, and generally knew everything about this 'body-politic' as a good companion should! Dutifully following my lead, Anaphielian was looking forward to his companion, too.

–Oh, here she is, my lord. Anaphielian, look and see. This is a teenager. A car accident claimed her over to Death Incarnate's capable hands. Have you made arrangements with Him to give the souls back over to the living world?

Anaphielian spoke.

–Tiperia made those arrangements already, I understand. This is a magic spell, and that's why Clareina is here, I'm here for backup and I'm going to get companionized right away! Should be fun.

Clareina gave a wink.

Jing was very calm. The guards were put immediately to sleep, again a nod to Clareina. She was using magic with abandon. Joan looked at the dead girl and waited.

–Everything depends on Joan. Is this the girl that will be your companion, my companion?

Joan had no racism about her whatever. That's my companion for you, yes, I'll just keep her, annoying, little Universe be still!

–That's her, my lord. I feel it in my <u>heart</u> which is still one with God!

–Appropriately worded, now I can rid myself of this little thing, come forth, Darcey!

The heart-shaped box I ripped off and put over the girl's chest.

---

should have used more caution dealing with Danillia. Now there are different perspectives about the 'quest-for-saurian-muscle,' but these are Anakimian's words, and no other! Take them or don't!

Everyone was naked in this morgue, which is no big deal to me, my gorgeous birthday suit not withstanding.

Clareina performed her spell, the girl, Darcey, was instantly awake.

–Oh, my lord! It was just a moment. I didn't feel anything, wow. This, this is my…new body?

Clareina was now concerned.

–If it isn't to your liking, we can—

–No, no, it is very suitable. I feel great!

–Not as great as you're going to feel. This is your companion Anaphielian.

–And I can help with any magic spell, Clareina, at your service!

The mega-Velociraptor Darcey now saw widened her eyes. She liked Anaphielian right off!

At length, Joan had a look back into the room with all the dead bodies. She felt a longing, and I was immediately at her side, nodding.

–What is it my child? What concerns you so?

–I just wish, oh—

–Just say it, my companion, don't worry, continue?

–I wish all could be awaked, and away from death, my lord.

Clareina, Anaphielian and I looked on with open mouths, which is a sight, according to Brian, remarking on our teeth. Darcey and Jing looked at us, too, and nodded.

–We are not God Almighty, mind, just your local neighborhood gods, and that's with a small "g" alright?

The human companions then shrugged and got together and hugged. Jing, Darcey and Joan, a special kind of 'commitment' was contained in that little hug, you could just see it.

Touched, we three dragon-stars held back a little, looking at the morgue. Then we traveled to Florida as dragons, making off with our friend-companions, Katrina riding Clare back (nay, her strapping, sinuous non-sexy-back!)

Small 'g' in gods, yes, my friends, you humans got that? Well, good. However, in <u>this</u> Florida morgue, there was movement. Just a little, but movement all the same. Fingers immobile and life-gone, was returned. The sheets fell on the floor, that once covered bodies-many. Stirring began. There <u>are</u> second chances to this life. Maybe 'second chances' is <u>everything</u> said.

FINIS

Printed in the United States
By Bookmasters